To Robby and
Becky.
august 24, 1978

THE BOBBSEY TWINS AND
THE TAGALONG GIRAFFE

A TRIP to Africa, home of lions, giraffes, hippos and gazelles, brings the Bobbsey Twins face to face with their most exciting adventure. Who are the bad men stealing defenseless wild animals? How can they be stopped? Bob Buyanda, head of the Kenya Rangers, may have the answers. But after delivering a gift package to the Bobbseys, he disappears. How the Bobbsey Twins, with only a handful of clues, solve a mystery and deal with the animal poachers is a story you won't want to miss.

The long trunk came through the opening.

The Bobbsey Twins and the Tagalong Giraffe

By

LAURA LEE HOPE

GROSSET & DUNLAP
A National General Company
Publishers   *New York*

PRINTED IN THE UNITED STATES OF AMERICA
LIBRARY OF CONGRESS CATALOG CARD NO. 72-92932
ISBN: 0-448-8066-4
The Bobbsey Twins and the Tagalong Giraffe

CONTENTS

THE BOBBSEY TWINS AND
THE TAGALONG GIRAFFE

CHAPTER I

AN AFRICAN SURPRISE

"FREDDIE, Flossie, come quickly!" twelve-year-old Nan Bobbsey called out the back door. "We have a surprise."

In the snow-covered yard the six-year-old twins hopped off their sleds and ran toward the house.

"What is it?" asked Freddie. Blond hair peeked from under his red hat and his cheeks were rosy with the cold.

"Something about as tall as you are. And it has spots."

"Where did it come from?" asked Flossie as they clomped into the kitchen and kicked off their boots.

"Africa," replied Nan. "The expressman brought it."

"What can it be?" wondered Flossie. They followed Nan to the front hall.

There Bert Bobbsey, Nan's dark-haired twin, was kneeling beside a wooden crate, holding it steady while his father opened the slats with a screwdriver.

"See the label?" asked Bert with a grin. Big letters on the side read: GIRAFFE.

Flossie's eyes grew wide. "A real live one?"

"Oh no," replied Mrs. Bobbsey, giving her little girl a hug. "It's a toy."

"Who's it from?"

"Tippy. Remember her?"

Freddie and Flossie clapped their hands. All the Bobbseys loved Tippy Martin, the young photographer they had met while on their *Baby May* adventure.

"She got married," Nan said. "Her name is Mrs. James Barton now."

Smiling, the twins recalled when they had "discovered" Tippy. It was just in time for her to claim the prize she had won in a photography contest—a trip around the world.

"If it hadn't been for us," said Flossie, "Tippy wouldn't have gone to Africa and met that nice newspaper reporter and married him."

Just then the last slat of the crate came off. There stood a yellow wooden giraffe with dark brown spots. Around its neck was a red Christmas bow with an envelope attached. It was addressed to: The Bobbsey Twins. Bert opened it and read the note out loud:

"Dear twins, how would you like to come to Africa and solve a mystery?"

"Oh! Would we!" exclaimed Freddie.

Bert read on: *"Jim and I are inviting you to spend your Christmas holidays with us on a safari."*

"On a what?" asked Flossie.

"Safari," said Bert. "That's an African word. It means a trip, usually to hunt or photograph wild animals."

"Oh, it sounds like fun!" exclaimed Nan.

"There's more," said Bert. *"At the same time you could keep an eye on Twiga. Your mother and father will tell you all about it. Love, Tippy."*

"Mommy!" exclaimed Freddie. "What does she mean?"

Mr. and Mrs. Bobbsey exchanged smiles. "I really don't know about Twiga," their mother said. "But Daddy and I have been keeping a secret. We're all going to Africa for Christmas."

"Africa! Oh boy!" Freddie jumped up and down and did a cartwheel, nearly knocking Nan over.

Flossie threw her arms around her mother, while Bert was one big grin.

Mr. Bobbsey explained that Tippy had written the grownups a week before. "The main reason for the safari is to try to catch a gang of poachers," he said.

Flossie giggled. "Do they poach eggs? I like scrambled better."

Mr. Bobbsey laughed and said the poachers were bad men who stole animals from the national parks in East Africa. He added, "A very clever African detective is in charge of this trip. His name is Bob Buyanda. He's a friend of the Bartons."

"Tippy and Jim are going along," Mrs. Bobbsey said, "to take photographs and write an article about the animals. Mr. Buyanda will be their driver. And with you in the party, the trip will look like an innocent children's safari. The gang will never suspect there are five detectives after them!"

"Tippy has told Mr. Buyanda about you," their father added, "and he's hoping you'll help him."

"We will!" exclaimed Nan.

"Daddy and I can't come with you, though," Mrs. Bobbsey went on.

"Oh, why not?" Freddie asked, disappointed.

"Not enough room. But we're taking a tourist safari to the same two countries you'll visit —Kenya and Tanzania. And we'll be going to the same national parks."

"So we'll see each other sometimes," said Mr. Bobbsey with a smile.

"When are we leaving?" Bert asked.

"In three weeks. The plans are all made. We'll start the safari from Nairobi, where Tippy lives. Your principal has given permission for a longer Christmas vacation."

At that moment, a large, pleasant-faced woman in a pink apron came down the stairs carrying a bag of laundry.

"Dinah!" cried Flossie. "We're going to Africa!"

"I know, honey. The land of my ancestors. I wish I could come, too!"

Dinah Johnson and her husband Sam had lived with the family ever since the older twins were born. Dinah helped Mrs. Bobbsey with the housekeeping, and Sam worked at Mr. Bobbsey's lumberyard.

"I'm going to take my new lasso, Dinah," said Bert with a twinkle in his eyes. "Shall I catch a lion for you?"

Dinah laughed. "No sirree! I don't want any lion in my kitchen!" Chuckling, she went on down the hall.

"There's just one thing," Mrs. Bobbsey said. "Danny Rugg and his father have signed up to go on our safari."

"Oh, oh. Bad news," said Bert.

Danny was Bert's age and the neighborhood bully. He liked to make trouble for the Bobbseys whenever he could.

"Don't worry," said Nan. "We may not see much of him."

A few minutes later the young twins went outdoors again with their camera to play make-believe safari. The family's two dogs ran around the corner of the house. One was brown, the other white.

"Here, Waggo, here, Snap!" called Freddie. "You can be elephants."

But the dogs disappeared around the other corner.

"They don't want to play," said Flossie. "But look, Freddie, there's a lion!"

"It's the first black-and-white lion I ever saw," Freddie remarked as the Bobbseys' cat, Snoop, leaped off the back porch rail.

The children followed, snapping pictures of the cat. Snoop ran to the tree beside the garage, scooted up the trunk, and dropped to the garage roof.

"I know it's dangerous," said Freddie, trying to sound like a grown-up camera hunter, "but I'm going closer."

"Watch yourself," whispered Flossie. "That lion's ready to spring!"

Freddy hung the camera around his neck and climbed up the drainpipe to the steeply sloping garage roof.

When he stepped onto the edge, Snoop backed up, arched her back and hissed. Freddie quickly snapped a picture.

"What a dopey shot!" came a loud voice. Danny Rugg appeared behind Flossie. He wore a green jacket and was making a big snowball. The next moment he threw it at Freddie.

"Ow!" the little boy yelled as the ball hit him on the ear. He slipped, sat down hard and slid off the roof in a shower of snow!

Freddie landed in a deep drift and the camera flew from his hand. Danny caught it and darted off.

"Give it back!" cried Flossie.

"Try and make me!" Danny ran down the drive, snapping picture after picture of nothing in particular. When he reached the front walk he tossed the camera to Freddie.

"Here—catch!" he called and ran off, laughing.

"He used up all my film," said Freddie angrily. The young twins went into the house and found Bert practicing in the basement with his lariat. They told him what had happened.

"His father should pay for a new roll of film," Bert said hotly. "Well, I'll bet you and Flossie got some good shots. What kind of film do you have?"

"For slides. The kind Daddy can throw on the screen."

"Maybe we could take them to Africa with us," said Flossie, "to show Tippy's husband. He's never seen Snoop."

"That would be keen," said Freddie, cheering up.

For the next three weeks the family was busy

Freddie slid off the roof in a shower of snow!

preparing for the trip. The wooden giraffe stood next to the hall table. Every time Flossie passed it, she patted it on the head. "We're going to see your relatives," she sang.

Finally the day came. Dinah kissed all the children good-by in the front hall and Sam drove the family to the airport in the Bobbseys' station wagon.

"Have a good time now," he said as he shook hands with everyone at the ticket counter. He was a tall, cheerful man who liked to joke. But today he looked a little sad.

"Dinah and I will miss you," he said.

"We'll miss you, too, Sam," said Nan, and Flossie gave him a parting hug.

An hour later the travelers were in the airplane flying across the Atlantic Ocean toward Spain. Danny Rugg passed their seats several times, but only made faces. Mr. Rugg, a stout, tired-looking man, kept a close eye on his son.

It was night when they landed in Madrid. The family was driven to a hotel near the airport and, early next morning, boarded another plane. Several hours later they landed in Casablanca.

"Now we're in Africa," said Bert to the young twins.

They changed at once to a larger airplane.

"This will be a long trip," said Nan. "We have to cross Africa from west to east."

As the hours went by the children read and

played games. Part of the time they looked down and watched the Congo River winding like a silver snake through the dark green of the forests. At last the pilot announced Lake Victoria. The Bobbseys looked out again to see a large lake shining in the moonlight.

"There's a famous falls here," said Bert. "Both it and the lake are named for an English Queen."

It was late at night when the huge aircraft landed at Nairobi. The weary travelers took a taxi along dark, quiet roadways to a hotel in the city.

When Mr. Bobbsey had registered, the desk clerk said, "There's a package here for the children." He handed a medium-sized carton to Nan. "Mr. Bob Buyanda left it for you."

"That's the detective," remarked Bert. "I wonder what's in it."

The family followed a bellhop into an elevator and rode to the third floor. Nan was last in line walking down a dim corridor. Suddenly a man darted out of an open door. He was of average height, and had a pale, puffy face.

Without a word, the fellow grabbed the package from Nan's hands and raced down the hall.

"Stop!" Nan screamed.

CHAPTER II

THE MYSTERIOUS TWIGA

"STOP, thief!" Nan cried again. Startled, the others turned just in time to see the man disappear around a corner.

"After him!" exclaimed Bert. He and Nan dashed down the corridor with their family and the bellhop close behind. As the Bobbseys rounded the corner, they saw the man step into an open elevator. Before they could reach him, the doors closed.

"He's going down!" Bert shouted. "Come on! Maybe we can catch him in the lobby!"

The Bobbseys raced down two flights of stairs and reached the lobby. It was empty, except

11

for the clerk behind the desk. Mr. Bobbsey hastened up and explained what had happened.

"The elevator came down," the clerk confirmed, "but the only person to come out was a short, fat woman!"

"The thief must have got off on another floor," Bert said, disappointed.

When Nan described the man, the clerk promised to keep an eye out for him, and also to report the theft to the police.

"I wonder why he wanted the package," said Bert. "Do you have any idea what was in it?"

"No," the clerk replied. "But Mr. Buyanda said it was important."

Again the bellhop took them in the elevator back to the third floor and showed the family into two large, cheerful rooms.

"We must get a good night's rest," said Mrs. Bobbsey. "Tomorrow we're invited to Tippy's for lunch and we have tickets for a tour in the afternoon."

"I can't wait to see Tippy," said Nan happily.

"And find out who or what Twiga is," Flossie added.

Next morning at eleven the Bobbseys set out in two cabs. Flossie and Freddie wore matching yellow shorts and tops with orange beanies. Bert wore tan, while Nan had on a blue outfit.

"What a pretty place Nairobi is," said Nan as they rode down a flower- and tree-lined street.

Soon they passed a large white building with two towers. On top of each was a lacy white dome.

"That's a mosque," Bert said. "It's a place where Moslem people worship."

The driver, a thin, dark-skinned man, spoke up. "We have churches, too. People of many different nationalities, races, and religions live here."

They passed several East Indian women wearing beautiful saris of pink and blue. Some men wore business suits and hats, others had turbans. Many women wore high Afro hair styles with short bright-colored dresses. The majority of the people were black.

"Why does everybody drive on the wrong side of the street?" asked Freddie.

"Kenya used to belong to England," said the driver, "and in that country the left side of the road is the right side!"

Presently both taxis drew up before a small white villa. Bright purple flowers were growing on a vine over the front porch.

As the Bobbseys stepped out of the taxis, the front door burst open and a pretty young woman in a green dress came out.

"Tippy!" cried Flossie.

The twins ran to meet their friend as she hurried across the lawn, her long red hair streaming in the breeze. Behind her was a tall, good-looking man whose hair was red, too.

"Oh, I'm so glad to see you!" exclaimed Tippy. She hugged the excited children and for a few minutes there was happy confusion while the taxi drivers were paid and everyone talked at once.

Then Tippy introduced her husband. He smiled and shook hands with all the visitors. "Please call me Jim," he said in a crisp, English accent.

Beaming, his wife led the way inside the house. The living room was cool and decorated with green plants and flowers. As soon as everyone was seated, Bert told the Bartons about the stolen package.

"Do you know what was in it?" Nan asked Jim, "or why anyone would want to take it?"

The newsman looked worried. "I don't know. But I'm afraid this means trouble for our safari."

He said that Bob Buyanda was well known in Nairobi because he had done such a fine job of catching poachers in the past. "It may be that the new gang is spying on him."

"And the spy wanted to find out what Mr. Buyanda left for the children," said Mrs. Bobbsey.

"Now the poachers know that Mr. Buyanda is connected with us," said Bert, frowning. "That means they'll be watching us."

"It's possible," Mr. Bobbsey remarked, "but we can't be sure. The man may have been an ordinary thief."

"Besides," Jim added, "even if the gang is onto our plan, we can trust Bob to work out a solution. He's a ranger as well as a detective and a very clever man."

"That's why the governments of Kenya and Tanzania wanted him to take on this job," Tippy added. She explained that the poachers were working in the national parks of both countries. "They're called the Leopard Gang," she said, "because they are very hard to see or catch and they strike at night."

"It is the same with real leopards," said Jim. He explained that hunting in the parks was forbidden. "These men shoot their prey with sedative guns."

"You know," Nan said to the young twins, "instead of a bullet out comes a tiny hypodermic needle. It injects medicine which puts the animals to sleep for a while."

"Then they're hauled away and sold to zoos," Jim went on. "Others may be killed for their hides and horns."

"Oh, those mean old meanies!" Flossie exclaimed.

"If the animals are not protected from poachers, they will be wiped out," Jim went on.

"How sad that would be," said Nan. "No more lions or elephants or anything."

"Mr. Buyanda will see that it doesn't happen," Jim said. "We'll telephone him tonight and tell him about the stolen package. He won't be home until evening."

"Tippy," Flossie spoke up. "Please tell us—who's Twiga?"

"Oh, Twiga. Jim will show you."

Grinning, the Englishman led his guests down a hallway, through a bright yellow kitchen and out onto a stone patio.

Beyond lay a lawn bordered with rows of tall, bright red poinsettias. Jim pointed to a wire pen at the far end. "There she is!"

"A little giraffe!" exclaimed Flossie. The children raced across the grass toward the baby animal with the others following.

"Twiga, old girl," Jim said, "meet the Bobbseys." The giraffe bent her head and the twins gently patted her neck.

"Oh, she's darling!" Nan exclaimed. "Look at those big dark eyes and long lashes!"

"Where did you get her?" asked Bert.

"Park rangers found her lying on the ground some time ago," Jim replied. "She had been shot by poachers, but they left her behind in their hurry. She was brought to the animal nursery here in Nairobi to recover."

As he spoke, Tippy arrived with a tray of glasses filled with pineapple juice and a basket of crackers.

"Let me help," said Nan and began passing the basket.

"We brought Twiga here yesterday," Tippy said, "so I could take some pictures of her in our garden. Jim built the pen for her."

"Tomorrow she goes on safari with us," Jim said. "We're taking her back to her native park, Masai Mara in Tanzania. She has to learn to live in the wild again."

With that, the young animal put down her head and took a cracker from the basket.

Everyone laughed. "She just loves them," said Tippy. "The keepers fed her crackers for a treat."

The next moment the giraffe bent down again and lifted Flossie's beanie off her head!

"There goes your hat!" exclaimed Bert and everyone burst out laughing.

"Drop it, Twiga!" said Bert.

The animal looked at him, slowly blinked her soft brown eyes and dropped the hat.

"Twiga is Swahili for giraffe," said Jim. "Most East Africans speak Swahili."

"She ought to have an American name, too," remarked Freddie.

"Let's call her Crackers," Flossie suggested.

"That's a good idea," said Tippy. "Now you have two names, Twiga!"

Later the Bobbseys' pretty young hostess served a delicious lunch of fruit salad and freshly baked rolls at a large table on the patio. Over the dessert of banana shortcake, they all made exciting plans for the next day.

Finally, Mrs. Bobbsey glanced at her watch and said they had to leave. "We mustn't miss our tour," she explained.

"There goes your hat!" exclaimed Bert.

Taxis were called and before long the Bobbseys were on their way. As they pulled up in front of the hotel, they saw a group of people waiting to get into two small black-and-white striped zebra buses.

"We're just in time," said Mr. Bobbsey.

When the family reached the first bus there was not enough room for all of them.

"Some of you come in here," called the driver of the second bus. It was like a large car inside and had no aisle. He put Bert and Freddie into the wide back seat, each by an open window. A few minutes later, the Ruggs arrived. Mr. Rugg was placed in front and Danny between the Bobbseys.

"You boys can take turns at the windows," said the driver. "I'll tell you when to change."

Just then a tall, thin man in dark glasses took the seat in front of the boys. As the bus drove to the outskirts of town he spoke to no one. Soon they passed through a gateway into Nairobi National Park.

"The rules are strict," the driver warned them. "We must not annoy the animals. We cannot chase them, honk the horn, or leave the car at any time."

At first the tourists saw only trees and grass. Then they exclaimed in excitement. Lying under a tree was a large lion with a magnificent mane!

The bus bounced off the road, crossed the

grass and stopped a few yards from the beast. He blinked sleepily as everyone began taking pictures.

"I want to sit there!" said Danny, pulling on Freddie, who clung to the window ledge.

"Keep your hands off my brother!" said Bert. "It's not your turn yet!"

As he dragged Danny away, the bully knocked him against the passenger in front.

"Oh!" said the startled man. He pitched forward and his glasses flew out the window!

CHAPTER III

BAD NEWS

THE man turned to the boys, his long face red with anger.

"I'm sorry," said Bert. "But it wasn't my fault!"

"I saw the whole thing in the mirror," the driver cut in. "That boy in the middle will have to sit down and wait his turn."

"And who's going to pay for my glasses?" asked the tall man. They were lying in the grass in front of the lion.

Mr. Rugg, who had been scolding his son and was just as angry as the tall man, said, "Don't worry, I'll take care of it." He took out his wallet and paid him enough money for new sunglasses.

"This will be deducted from your allowance," Mr. Rugg said to Danny. "There's always trouble when you and the Bobbseys are together," he added with a sigh. "I just hope we won't be on the same tour bus."

"Our mother and father will be with you," Freddie replied politely, "but we won't. We're going on a special safari."

"Oh boy, do you think you're smart!" sneered Danny. "Is this another one of your stupid detective trips?"

"Detectives?" the tall man said and turned around. Now he was smiling. "Aren't you a little young for that?"

"It's true, though," Mr. Rugg admitted. "The Bobbsey Twins often catch thieves."

"Is that so?" the stranger spoke pleasantly, but his small black eyes were sharp. "Are you working on a case now?"

"We came to Africa to see the animals," replied Bert quietly.

Freddie took the hint and said nothing. The man asked more questions but Bert avoided giving him any further information.

As the ride went on, the tourists eagerly photographed the animals—sleek, spotted cheetahs, hundreds of antelope, plump zebras, and many others. Danny was so interested that he behaved for the rest of the tour. Only the tall man did not seem thrilled by the marvelous display of nature.

"I wonder why he came," Bert thought.

Back at the hotel, the family gathered in the lounge before dinner. They talked excitedly about the wild animals and of the safari to start the following day.

At ten o'clock next morning the Bobbseys were on the sidewalk in front of the hotel with all their luggage. Flossie was holding some boxes of crackers she had bought for the giraffe.

"Our safari leaves a little while after yours," Mr. Bobbsey said. "We'll have dinner with you tonight at Amboseli Game Reserve."

"Have fun now," Mrs. Bobbsey said as she hugged Flossie and Freddie.

A landrover arrived, pulling a small open trailer with Twiga. Jim sat beside the driver, a handsome black man. In the back seat were Tippy and a young black boy.

With a frown Jim got out of the car, and instantly the Bobbseys felt something was wrong.

"Oh dear, what's happened?" asked Mrs. Bobbsey.

"Bad news," Jim replied. "Bob Buyanda has disappeared! No one has seen him since yesterday afternoon."

Bert thought immediately of the Leopard Gang but said nothing.

"Has our safari been called off?" asked Freddie.

"No," Jim replied. "Bob's brother will take over." He beckoned to the driver, who left the landrover and came over. He wore a white shirt and dark trousers.

"This is Richard Buyanda," said Jim and introduced the Bobbseys. "He's a ranger, too."

The man shook hands with the visitors. "You may call me Richard," he said in a deep, musical voice. He turned to the boy, who had followed him out of the car. "This is my son Billy. He's going, too."

"That's keen," said Bert, and Billy nodded shyly.

"Billy's fourteen," Tippy told them. "He's going to be a ranger, too. He already knows a lot about African wildlife."

As the men stowed the bags in the landrover, Billy led the twins to the back of it. There was just enough room between the car and the trailer for him to let down the door.

All the children climbed in and sat along the sides facing each other. Tippy was on the wide seat in front with camera equipment, the baggage, and a box of emergency rations.

Jim shut the door, then got in beside Richard. As the caravan started, the twins and their parents waved and called good-by.

"Hello, Crackers," said Freddie, looking out the open back window at the giraffe.

"We heard about her new name," said Billy, smiling.

As the landrover and the trailer threaded through traffic, the boy explained that he had been excused from school to help find his uncle. "The police are looking for him, too," he added.

"What do you suppose happened to him?" asked Nan.

"I think the poachers found out about our safari," Billy replied, "and kidnapped him before he could come after them."

"It sounds likely," Bert agreed.

"Jim told us about the stolen package," added Richard, "but we don't know what was in it."

After reaching open fields they passed a tall native man walking down the road carrying a spear. He wore a long, dull red cloth draped over one shoulder like a toga. His hair was in many thin braids and smeared with reddish paint.

"He is a Masai," said Billy as the three Africans waved to one another. "He belongs to the same tribe as we do."

Flossie looked surprised. "But you're not dressed like that."

"No. Mother, Dad, Uncle Bob and I live in a house in Nairobi, so we wear city clothes."

A few minutes later Richard pointed out a circle of long mud huts with rounded roofs. Around it was a thick hedge of dry branches. "There's a Masai village," Richard said. "That's a fence of thorns to keep out lions."

About noon the safari turned up a side road into Amboseli Game Reserve. At first there were scattered trees, then open ground. Far away the children saw herds of buffalo. Dozens of dainty little antelope sprang along beside the car.

"Those are Thompson's Gazelles," said Billy. "We call them tommies."

It was early in the afternoon when the land-rover drove through a stone gateway up to an attractive lodge. On the lawn was a swimming pool filled with sparkling water.

Richard explained that he and his son would stay in the drivers' quarters at each hotel. "That way no one will suspect that we are anything but a regular safari driver and his helper."

"What about Crackers?" asked Flossie.

"There are pens or sheds at all the lodges where she can be housed," the ranger replied.

Ten minutes later the travelers were settled in one of the double guest cabins behind the main building. Jim and the boys took one side, Tippy and the girls the other.

After lunch, Bert, Freddie, and Billy wandered around the lounge. Suddenly Bert said, "Look who's here, Freddie!"

Seated on a leather sofa was the unfortunate man who had lost his sunglasses the day before. He wore a new pair, which looked even darker, and seemed not to notice the three boys.

"I suppose he's touring Africa like you," Billy remarked. "I've never seen him before."

"We met him yesterday," Bert said and told Billy the story.

A little later Nan slipped into the gift shop in the lobby. In the window were some carved wooden animals. One was a lion, his mouth open in a roar.

"That would be great for Bert's Christmas gift," she thought and asked the man behind the counter, "May I look at the animals?"

He took off his steel-rimmed glasses and smiled. "Help yourself!"

As Nan picked up the smooth, brown carving, the man with the sunglasses came through the doorway. Without a word, he snatched the lion from her hand, looked at the bottom, gave it back to her and strode out of the shop.

"What was that all about?" asked the clerk.

"I don't know," Nan replied. She handed the wooden animal to him and paid the price marked on a sticker.

"Funny," he said as he wrapped the carving. "I checked all the wooden animals when I opened today. This lion wasn't among them."

"Then how did it get into the window?" Nan asked.

The man shrugged. "When I was out for lunch, somebody must have put it there. My boss, perhaps."

"It's a mystery lion," Nan thought as she went out of the shop and joined the others.

The twins spent the rest of the afternoon at the pool with Billy. As they splashed in the cool water, their new friend pointed to a snow-capped peak miles away across a plain. "That's Mount Kilimanjaro," he said. "The highest mountain in Africa. We're lucky to see all of it. The peak is often lost in the clouds."

That evening the two safaris met and everyone had dinner together.

Nan reported the incident in the gift shop and how strange the man with the sunglasses had acted.

"From your description of the man, I think we know him," Mrs. Bobbsey said. "We met him a little while ago. His name is Arthur Needles. And he asked a lot of questions about your safari. The whole thing is really odd."

"He's traveling with a man named Ernest Soper," Mr. Bobbsey put in. "They're driving a rented car and they are following the same route we are."

"Maybe Mr. Needles is just a busybody," said Jim. "But we'd better keep an eye on him."

"I've got a feeling that he's keeping an eye on *us*," Bert remarked.

That night, when the girls were in their pajamas, Nan examined the carved lion. On the bottom was blurred writing in red ink.

"Looks like a number 8 and then a word starting with j," she thought and showed it to her sister and Tippy.

The man snatched the lion from Nan's hand.

They examined the carving carefully, but no one could make out the red marks.

"Well, we'd better get to bed now," Tippy said. "We'll have a long day tomorrow."

In the other half of the cabin, the boys were already asleep. About midnight Bert awoke feeling thirsty. As he sat up, he glanced out the window. Moving across the lawn was a blinking green light!

CHAPTER IV

A ROARING LIONESS

BERT shook Freddie and Jim. "Wake up!"

Jim bounded to his feet. "What happened?"

"Look!" Bert said and pointed to the blinking green light across the lawn. "I think somebody is signaling." The three watched intently, but it was too dark to see anything except the light.

"Maybe it's for the poachers," suggested Freddie.

"Could be," said Jim. "I think we'd better alert Richard." The next moment the light vanished.

Bert dressed, attached his lariat and flashlight to his belt, and hurried next door. He told the girls about the strange signal. Flossie and

Tippy were out on their porch in slippers and robes when Freddie and Jim ran up.

"I'll go with you," Nan said, coming out in blue jeans and a sweater.

"Okay," said Jim. "You young twins stay with Tippy. Watch to see if the light comes again."

The older children and Jim hastened past the guesthouses toward a long, low frame building where the drivers slept. As Bert rounded one of the outlying sheds, someone grabbed his arm.

Bert struck out, but at that instant recognized Billy.

"Easy!" whispered the African boy. "I was coming for you. Did you see the light?"

"Yes. That's why we're here."

"Where's your father?" asked Jim.

"Over in the parking lot—using the radio in our landrover to call the rangers. He thinks someone might have been signaling the poachers."

As the four went on through the dark, Billy explained that because of the Leopard Gang there was a special poacher patrol operating in each of the national parks.

"These rangers are based at the hotels," he said. "They don't wear uniforms and they use zebra buses as well as landrovers. That way, no one can tell them from regular tourist drivers."

"I didn't know we had a radio in our car," said Nan.

"There are no telephones out here in the wild," Billy replied. "People use radios to keep in touch with one another."

Reaching the landrover, they found Richard working over the set in the front seat.

"Something's wrong," he said, looking worried. "There are ten cars covering Amboseli. None of them answers my call."

"We'd better find one," Jim suggested.

"Right. Let's go!"

The twins climbed into the back with Billy and Jim slid in the front next to Richard. The trailer was no longer attached, and the African drove without lights through the gate.

"Where are you heading, Dad?" asked Billy.

"For the north clearing. The tourist drivers reported a lot of tommies in that area late this afternoon. I'm sure a ranger car will be stationed there to watch for the poachers."

After several bumpy miles, the landrover swerved from the dirt road and started an even bumpier drive across country. The moon had risen and the searchers could see odd trees with wide flat tops like parasols.

"Those are thorn trees," Billy told the Bobbseys.

"Look!" Bert cried suddenly. "Lights!" He pointed to a woods half a mile ahead.

As the landrover bounced closer, there came some shouts and two men ran out waving flashlights.

"Rangers!" Richard exclaimed. "I recognize their voices!"

He opened the window and called out to the men, who had almost reached the car.

"We've been tricked!" one of them said. His deep voice was angry. "The poachers have slipped through our fingers!"

"What happened?" Jim asked.

"My partner and I were patroling in our zebra bus when we saw lights over in the gully." He pointed some distance away to a line of bushes that led into a grove of tall trees.

"We parked in the woods," the second ranger said, "crept up and eavesdropped on two men hiding in the ditch. We heard them say the gang would meet in that grove of big trees. They expected about fifty baboons there."

"We ran back to our bus," the first man continued, "and radioed the other rangers. In twenty minutes all our cars were hidden in this little woods. Then we sneaked up on the grove."

"And nothing happened," Bert guessed.

"Right. We waited awhile, then came back and found all the radios smashed and the car batteries stolen."

"That's bad," Jim spoke up. "It means the gang stranded you all here and went on to strike somewhere else—maybe in the north clearing."

"I'll radio the lodge to send you help," Richard said. "Then we'll see if we can find the poachers. If we hurry we may not be too late to stop them."

"You can't tackle them alone," said the deep-voiced man.

"I know. But we may be able to scare them off."

Moments later the landrover was rattling across the moonlit plain toward the area in which small antelope had been sighted in the afternoon. After passing through a wooded section, the searchers came into a large clearing.

"It's so bright with the full moon shining," Nan said. "I hope the poachers don't see us!"

"We're too late!" Richard said grimly. "Look at the ground!"

The earth was heavily trampled. Broken branches of brush lay around the edges of one end of the clearing. Richard pointed to long, wide marks among the shoe and hoof marks. "That's where the thieves dragged the animals away."

"There must have been a lot of them," Nan remarked sadly.

Suddenly they heard a high, odd whistle.

"That's Uncle Bob's special signal!" Billy exclaimed. "He's around here somewhere!"

"Quiet," his father replied, but he sounded excited, too. "I'll look into it. The rest of you wait here."

"It could be a trick," Bert cautioned.

"I know. Billy, give me the rifles."

The boy took two guns from a locker under one of the rear seats and handed them to his father. Richard gave one to Jim, and kept the other. Then he swung out of the car, crossed the clearing, and disappeared among the trees.

Time crept by slowly for the group in the landrover. Finally, after what seemed an eternity, Billy said, "I'd better go look for Dad."

"No, stay in the car," said Jim. "I'll go."

The children watched until he disappeared into the woods. For a few minutes everything was quiet. Then they heard the deep roar of an animal.

"Wh-what was that?" Bert said. His knees shook a little.

"A lioness," Billy whispered. "Don't move."

A big beast came out from the trees. She stood still, her ears up, listening. The children sat like statues until the lioness melted away into the bush again.

"She's hunting," Billy remarked.

Suddenly Nan gasped and pointed to the other side of the clearing. A tiny gazelle came wobbling through the tall grass.

"A baby!" Nan exclaimed. "Where's its mother?"

"Maybe the poachers took her," replied Bert.

"Suppose the lioness comes back?" Nan was worried.

"That'll be the end of the tommie," Billy said. "Somehow we must get it into the car."

"I wish we could just get out and pick it up," Bert said.

"No!" Billy said firmly. "We can't take a chance like that!"

"I have an idea," Bert said. "I'll try to lasso it!" Quickly he took the lariat from his belt.

"Wait," Billy said. "The roof lifts up."

He opened two latches on the ceiling. Bert and Nan opened the others. Together they pushed up and the roof rose about two feet on metal struts. Then Bert crawled out the front opening and let himself down on the hood of the car.

As he started swinging the lasso around his head, the little antelope came closer on its shaky legs.

Suddenly the lioness roared nearby. The boy aimed carefully, tossed the rope and dropped the loop neatly around the animal's slender neck. Gently he began to pull the gazelle closer.

Suddenly the lioness appeared at the edge of the clearing.

"Bert!" Nan screamed.

Startled, her brother lost his balance and slipped off the hood onto the ground. At the same time the lioness began pacing toward them, her yellow eyes shining in the moonlight.

"Hurry, get in!" cried Nan, and Billy opened the car door. The great beast started to run. Bert jumped to his feet and scrambled inside, pulling the antelope with him.

"Hurry, get in!" Nan cried.

The lioness stopped short. Then she turned and trotted into the woods.

"Wow! That was close!" Billy said.

"You're telling me!" Bert shivered. "And don't scare me like that again, Nan!"

"This poor little thing is shaking," remarked the girl and cradled the baby gazelle in her arms.

Just then Jim and Richard appeared at opposite sides of the clearing. They met and talked a moment before walking up to the land-rover.

"We couldn't find a thing," Richard said. "That whistle is a mystery."

"Say," Jim remarked. "Where did you get the tommie?"

After the children had told of their scary adventure, Richard praised them and said, "We'll take the baby to the hotel. They'll send it to the animal nursery in Nairobi until it is strong enough to make it on its own out in the wilds."

"Oh, good," Nan said, and hugged the tommie.

It was nearly dawn when the party reached the lodge, weary from the night's futile search. By nine o'clock, the Bobbseys stood by the stone gate to say good-by to their parents. Bert was so sleepy that he could hardly keep his eyes open.

He noticed Mr. Needles at the wheel of a small blue car and yawned. The day was very hot and the man was mopping his brow, nodding to the elder Bobbseys.

Suddenly another man came through the gate. He wore a safari hat pulled low and held a handkerchief to his mouth, as he pushed past the group.

Bert's legs felt like rubber. He leaned against a pile of tourists' suitcases, lost his balance and fell. The bags toppled against the man. He sprawled forward and threw out his hands to break his fall. Mr. Bobbsey walked over and helped him to his feet again.

"Are you hurt?" he asked.

The man shook his head, mumbling, "Thank you." That was when Nan saw his face.

It was the thief who had snatched the package!

CHAPTER V

WHO IS SIMBA SAM?

BERT had picked himself up and noticed his sister was staring at the man, who nimbly hopped into the seat beside Mr. Needles.

"What's up, Nan?" he asked as the little car roared away.

"That man! He is the one who took our package!" Nan said.

Just then their parents were driving off in a zebra bus. Danny Rugg, who sat in the back, stuck out his tongue.

The twins turned back through the gate, where the Bartons stood talking to Richard and Billy on the patio beside the lodge. They hurried over and Nan told them about the man with the handkerchief.

"He must be Mr. Soper," Tippy said. "Mr. Needles' friend."

"Sure. And he held that handkerchief in front of his face because he was afraid Nan would recognize him!" Bert declared.

The detectives talked over their strategy. It would be easy enough to nab Needles and Soper.

"I've no doubt," Jim said, "that they're crooks, and that they are somehow connected with the poachers. But it's something we can't prove. Besides, we want to round up the whole kit and kaboodle at once. Nan, does Soper know you recognized him?"

Nan shrugged. "I can't say. Maybe not."

"Well, play it cool and make believe you didn't."

"They're headed for Lake Manyara," Richard put in. "I'll radio the Special Patrol there to be on the alert tonight. Meanwhile, Billy, you load Crackers into her trailer and the rest of you get ready to go!"

Half an hour later the landrover was on its way, with the giraffe rolling along behind. The radio was on the back seat between Bert and Billy.

"You boys are in charge of it," said Richard. "Keep it on in case the rangers want to reach us." As they rode, Billy showed the twins how to operate the equipment.

It was mid-morning when they passed through the gates of Amboseli again. They turned up the road and stopped at a white-washed building.

"This is where we leave Kenya and enter Tanzania," said Tippy.

Jim took all the travelers' passports into the house. Soon he was out again.

"Everything's okay," he said. A man in dark shorts and white shirt opened a long wooden barrier across the road and smilingly waved the party onward.

They drove for miles though green, rolling farmland. Now and then they saw neat-looking circles of huts.

"Tanzania is pretty," said Nan.

"What are those funny things?" asked Bert. He pointed to several red earth mounds with odd chimney-like tubes sticking up here and there.

"Anthills," Billy replied. "Some of them become very high—taller than my father."

Suddenly the radio crackled. There came high, clear pipe music. The travelers perked up their ears.

"Simba Sam here!" said a friendly male voice. "Welcome to the Bobbsey twins!"

The children were startled.

"How does he know our name?" asked Freddie.

"I don't know," said Billy, amazed.

"Where are you calling from?" Bert asked the stranger.

"Lake Manyara. The weather is sunny, but it may storm tonight. You'll pass some fine big herds of zebra when you come this way."

"But how do you know about us?" Bert pressed.

"Simba Sam knows all. Simba is Swahili for lion, you know. Would you like to learn a little Swahili?"

"Sure."

"All right. Repeat after me: Good morning —*jambo sana.*"

"*Jambo sana,*" chorused the Bobbseys.

"Good evening—*M'zuri sana.*"

Flossie giggled. "It sounds like the state of Missouri."

"Thank you," said their unseen friend, "is *asante,* and good-by is *kwaheri.*"

"Where do you live?" asked Jim. "What's your business?"

"I ride around safari country looking for you-know-who."

"What do you mean?"

"Good-by now," said the man cheerfully. "*Kwaheri!*"

"Wait!" Billy cried. But the man had signed off the air.

"Who in the world was that?" asked Tippy.

Jim shrugged. "I have no idea. Do you, Richard?"

"No. He sounded like a nice enough fellow."

"But how would he know about us unless he was connected with the crooks?" Bert reasoned.

"From what he said I thought he was *looking* for the crooks!" Nan argued.

"Maybe he's looking for Uncle Bob," Billy put in. "Uncle Bob has lots of friends in safari country."

"It sure is a puzzle," Nan said. "Was that a Masai pipe he was playing?"

"No," Richard replied. "Our people do not use pipes."

"Maybe Simba Sam is one of us and maybe not," remarked Billy.

"He sounded like an older man," said Tippy.

"Do you suppose we'll meet him at Lake Manyara?" Flossie asked.

Just then the car went over a deep rut. Everyone bounced hard.

"Ow!" cried Tippy as her head hit the roof.

"Are you hurt?" asked Nan worriedly.

"Not really," replied Tippy, "but I might raise a bump."

They rounded a bend and Richard said, "If you look straight ahead on the right you'll see an upside-down tree."

"An upside-down tree!" Flossie giggled.

"It's called that because its branches look like roots," Billy explained. He pointed to a huge gray tree trunk with a crown of crooked limbs.

"There it is," he said. "Its real name is Baobob tree."

As they passed, Flossie turned to watch it out the rear window. She let out a squeal of surprise. The trailer with the giraffe was gone!

"Stop!" the little girl cried. "We've lost Crackers!"

"Good grief!" Nan exclaimed. "The trailer must have broken loose when we went over that bump."

Quickly Richard turned the landrover around and drove back.

"There it is!" said Freddie as they rounded the bend again.

"But look!" Nan cried. "It's empty!"

"Oh, maybe a lion got her!" Flossie wailed.

"No, there she is!" Nan pointed to the giraffe's head sticking out above a clump of brush. "The trailer must have opened up and she just walked out."

"How do we get her back in?" Tippy asked.

"I've got some crackers," Flossie said, holding up the box she had brought.

"Good. Let's drive over," Richard said.

The big car bounced across the field and stopped close to the brush.

The giraffe watched quietly as the boys and Jim raised the roof. Flossie stood up on the seat and held a cracker through the opening. The animal reached over the brush, took the tidbit and ate it.

"Start driving, Dad," said Billy.

As the car moved slowly toward the road, the little giraffe followed, eating cracker after cracker. Finally they reached the trailer.

"Keep feeding her, Flossie," said Richard, which she did. The others got out of the car and circled the giraffe baby quietly. Then they gently but firmly steered her back into her cage.

From a toolbox under his seat Richard took a piece of chain and fastened the trailer to the landrover.

"You'd better tie the door closed, too," said Bert. "The catch is broken. The bump was too much for it."

Soon the safari was on its way once more. At noon they stopped in a small town for lunch, then Richard drove across a wild valley. It was covered with zebras!

"Simba Sam was right!" Tippy said. "Oh, Jim, what a beautiful picture!" She slung two cameras around her neck, and when Richard stopped she snapped a dozen pictures.

Four hours later the landrover wound up a steep road toward an attractive modern building on top of a cliff.

"That's the lodge where we'll stay," said Jim. He pointed to a dark green forest below and a large lake in the distance. "And there's the game reserve and Lake Manyara."

"The edge of that cliff would be a great place for someone to signal the poachers," said Bert. "We'd better keep watch there tonight."

"Good idea," Jim agreed.

Richard remarked that the Special Patrol was being doubled. "I've agreed to join them, but Jim can stake out the cliff top with Bert, Nan and Billy."

By the time they reached the hotel, their plans were made. While Jim registered for everyone, Tippy and the girls looked in the window of the gift shop, and the boys walked around the lobby.

"Nan! There's a roaring lion," Tippy said, "just like the one you bought for Bert."

As she spoke, Flossie spotted Mr. Needles standing at the desk. Quickly the trio drew behind two large potted plants and watched him intently.

After he had registered, he walked up to the gift shop and looked in the window. The clerk was waiting on another customer. Mr. Needles went inside, picked up the lion and glanced at the bottom. Then he quickly put it down again and left. Seconds later he was out of the girls' sight.

"Mr. Needles must like lions," Flossie remarked.

"There's more to it than that!" Nan said

The little giraffe followed, eating cracker after
cracker.

excitedly. "Maybe the gang leaves messages for him at the bottom of these carvings. Let's have a look—"

She was interrupted by the three boys, who came running toward them.

"A man just walked out of here," Freddie said breathlessly, "and Billy thinks it was his Uncle Bob. Come on, we've got to follow him."

Everyone bounded out the door, and Billy raced toward a tall, black man who strode down the long driveway to the parking lot below.

"Uncle Bob!" he cried, when they had almost reached him.

The man turned around. "Pardon me?"

Billy's face fell. "Oh, I—I'm sorry. I thought you were my uncle."

The man smiled. "I have a nephew, but he's a lot older than you." He waved and walked on.

Crestfallen, the group went back into the lobby. Nan told the boys about the lion. Bert and Freddie perked up immediately. "Hey, there's a red hot clue!" Bert said. "Let's find out what's on the bottom right now!"

They went back to the gift shop. Suddenly Nan let out a gasp. *The lion was gone!*

She rushed inside, followed by the others.

"May I help you, young lady?" the clerk asked.

"There was a carved lion in the window just a little while ago. What happened to it?"

"I sold it."

"To whom?"

"I can see you are American. But I did not expect the FBI!"

"Oh, please," Nan said. "It's important for us to find that particular lion."

"Sorry. It's gone. I can't remember who bought it, either. There were quite a few people in here just a little while ago."

"Thank you."

Nan was close to tears as they walked out. "Our red hot clue went right out the window!" she muttered.

"Not bad for a pun," Bert said, trying to cheer his sister up.

Nan could not help grinning. "I didn't mean it that way."

Just then Jim called for them to come, and soon they were settled in big, comfortable rooms with curtained glass doors at one end. Nan opened them and stepped out onto a balcony. A few feet below lay terraced gardens dotted with low green shrubs. Beyond, near the edge of the cliff, was a beautiful swimming pool.

"Hi, Freddie!" she called, looking toward the next balcony. Her brother came out.

"Mother and Daddy are here!" he announced. "They just telephoned. We're going to meet them for dinner."

The travelers washed and changed their clothes, then joined Mr. and Mrs. Bobbsey in the big dining room. While everyone enjoyed a hearty meal, the detectives told about their latest adventures and plans.

"Freddie, Flossie, and I will keep watch in the lobby," Tippy said.

"And if we see Mr. Needles or Soper heading for the cliff, I'll run out to the terrace and give a whistle signal for Bert and the others," added Freddie.

By the time it was dark, Bert, Nan, Jim, and Billy were hidden along the cliff edge, each behind some brush. For a long time nothing happened. Then, as the moon came out of a cloud, Nan spotted a crouching figure creeping up silently behind Jim.

"Jim!" she shouted. "Watch out!"

Instantly a strong hand grabbed her and another was clamped over her mouth!

Nan let out a muffled cry!

CHAPTER VI

FRIGHT IN THE NIGHT

AS Nan struggled, a blanket was thrown over her head. A rough hand stuffed a gag into her mouth, then she was tied up and pushed into a thicket.

Bert and Billy had been stationed some distance away and had heard the warning to Jim.

Billy made his way over to Bert. "Something's up. Let's go!"

Bert held his arm. "Better sneak up, though. If we run over there, the crooks'll grab us!"

As the two crept toward the spot where Jim had been hiding, they suddenly noticed a green light blinking!

"They're signaling again," Billy said. "The—"

"Shhh!" Bert interrupted. "Listen!"

A muffled groan came from behind a bush. The two sneaked up and found a small figure tied in a blanket. Quickly they opened the knots. "Nan!" her brother gasped.

Bert took the gag out of her mouth and motioned her to be silent. Then he whispered, "Are you all right?"

Nan nodded.

"What happened to Jim?"

"I don't know," Nan said. "He was over there and somebody was creeping up behind him. I yelled, and then they got me."

"Okay, come on," Billy said and led the way in the direction Nan had indicated.

They searched for Jim and finally found him lying against a tree down the cliffside. He was gagged and bound like Nan, and had a big bump on his head, a number of cuts and bruises on his arms, but otherwise was not seriously hurt.

"We saw the green light again," Billy reported tensely. "But it has stopped now."

"The poachers might strike tonight," Jim said grimly. "Billy, go down to the hotel radio room and get in touch with the patrol. We'll go toward the spot where the light came from. Maybe we can eavesdrop on the crooks."

"Okay." Billy vanished into the darkness,

and Nan and Bert followed Jim. They scoured the cliff for an hour. But there was no sign of the poachers.

"Let's go back to the hotel," Jim said finally. They did, and everyone gathered in the girls' room. Tippy examined the bump on Jim's head and looked at his cuts and bruises while he told what had happened.

Flossie went into the bathroom to get the first aid kit. She reached for the flat box on the shelf beside the wash basin.

Suddenly she thought, "That's funny. It's not dark in here and I didn't turn on the light." For the first time she noticed there was a wide open space all along the top of one wall. A glow of light from the corridor came into the bathroom. Then she heard a low, hoarse voice say:

"The Bobbseys are in these two rooms."

"We'd better get 'em out of the picture," another voice whispered. "That was a narrow escape tonight. They were watching for us."

"Don't worry, I have a plan," the first man announced.

Then there was silence. Bursting with excitement, Flossie rushed into the bedroom.

"The bad men are out in the hallway!" she exclaimed, and quickly told what she had heard.

Jim dashed to the door and opened it. Nobody was there. Jim ran down one side of the corridor, Bert the other. But they had no luck and returned to the room a few minutes later.

"I'll bet it was Needles and Soper," Bert said. "I wonder what they're planning."

"Let's see if there's any news in the radio room," Jim said and telephoned. But all was quiet. Richard and Billy had been in contact. Richard had seen the signal, too, and the poacher patrol was ready and waiting.

"All right now. Everybody to bed," Tippy said. "There's nothing more we can do, and you'll need your sleep."

The three girls were just dozing off, when a knock sounded on their door.

"Who's there?" Tippy called out.

"Jim. Open up."

In came the newsman and the boys, wearing robes and slippers.

"The radio room just phoned me," Jim said. "Tippy and I are to come down at once."

"Why?" Tippy asked.

"I don't know. We'll find out. I want all you children together in this room. Lock the door and open it to no one but us."

"Okay," the twins promised. After the Bartons had left, they sat on the beds listening for noises and discussing their adventure in low voices.

A few minutes later there was a scratching at the curtained balcony doors.

"What's that?" Freddie whispered.

Meow!

"It's a kitty!" Flossie said. Again the noise came, louder.

"Maybe the poor thing's hungry," said Nan. "We'd better let her in."

"What could we give her?" Flossie asked.

"Tippy has some cans of milk in her box of emergency rations."

Nan opened the door and they all looked out. *There was no cat in sight!*

"It must have jumped into the garden," said Freddie.

The kitten's cry came again farther off.

"Sounds as if it's in that big shrub over there," remarked Bert. He pointed to a low dark shape with a bunch of brush at the top.

"Let's try to find the kitty," Flossie begged.

"Okay," said Bert. "You and Nan come with me. Freddie, you stay here to open the door in case Tippy and Jim come back."

Bert climbed over the balcony railing onto the terrace. His sisters followed. While Freddie watched, the three walked quietly up to the bush.

"Here kitty, kitty," Flossie called softly.

The next instant she gasped in fright and grabbed Bert's arm.

The bush was growing taller!

The three froze as it rose like magic and loomed over them—a long dark shape with a bushy top!

"Mind your own business or you'll be sorry,"

it said in a quavery, spooky voice. The next moment it started moving toward them!

Too frightened to scream, Flossie turned and raced for the balcony. The older twins ran after her.

"Hurry, hurry!" shrieked Freddie. *"Don't let it catch you!"*

Bert helped his sisters onto the balcony, then glanced back at the weird thing. "This is some kind of trick," he thought.

Nan and Flossie burst into the room. "Come on, Bert, or it'll get you!" Flossie cried.

The boy raced into the room and she shut the glass door after him. The children looked through the curtains, their hearts beating fast. But the "bush" was retreating into the darkness, and soon they lost sight of it.

A knock sounded on the door to the hallway.

"Don't open it!" Bert said sharply. He walked over and called, "Who's there?"

"Jim. Let us in."

Bert opened the door and Jim and Tippy entered.

"Tippy, Tippy," cried Flossie and threw her arms around the girl. "We saw a walking bush!"

"What?"

Nan explained what had happened. Jim strode across the room and threw open the balcony doors. The garden was bathed in moonlight, and there was no sign of the fantastic figure.

"Hurry!" shrieked Freddie. "Don't let it catch you!"

"Someone wanted to scare us," Bert said.

"And succeeded," Jim said.

"What about the poor kitty?" asked Freddie.

"I don't think there was any cat," Nan declared. "Someone meowed to lure us outside."

"And the telephone message was a trick to get Jim and me out of the way," Tippy added. She explained that the people in the radio room had not sent for them at all.

"No news from the rangers yet," Jim said. "I'm beginning to think nothing will happen tonight after all."

Jim was right. In the morning, the travelers hurried to ask Richard if the poachers had been caught.

The ranger and his son were in front of the garage talking to a group of excited drivers.

"No luck last night," Richard said wearily to the Bobbseys. "Maybe the poachers found out the patrol was doubled and called the job off. But something else happened. One of our zebra buses was stolen!"

"Do you have any idea who took it?" Jim asked.

Richard shrugged. "Not the slightest."

A loud pounding came from a small shed next to the garage and Billy jumped up from the rock he had been sitting on.

"That's Crackers!" he exclaimed.

"Something's wrong!" Bert declared. "Come on!"

The twins and Billy ran around the corner of the shed. There stood Danny Rugg, poking a long stick through the open window. The frightened giraffe was kicking the wooden walls, trying to escape.

"Stop that. You're hurting the giraffe!" Bert cried.

CHAPTER VII

TRAPPED!

BERT yanked the stick away from Danny. "Get out of here and don't ever touch this giraffe again!"

"Who's going to stop me?" Danny taunted and dashed off.

"I am!" Bert ran after him. As Danny raced past the garage, he launched a flying tackle at him. Both boys hit the ground hard.

"Let me go!" yelled Danny, just as Richard and Jim came up.

"What's going on here?" Jim asked.

"Danny was hitting Crackers with a stick!" said Nan.

"You're a troublemaker, young man!" Jim declared and pulled Danny to his feet. "Now stay away from the Bobbseys and the giraffe!"

Danny slunk off without saying a word.

"Let's have breakfast," Jim said. "Then we're going down into the forest to photograph the animals."

They went into the dining room and joined Mr. and Mrs. Bobbsey, who had just ordered bacon and pancakes.

After breakfast, the elder Bobbseys said good-by, and the twins and their friends piled into the landrover with their cameras. The wind whipped the girls' hair as they roared down the hill with the roof raised, and passed out through the gate into the deep green forest.

Almost at once they saw a big baboon sitting on the end of a fallen log.

"Oh, wait!" exclaimed Tippy. "I want his picture!"

"He's got gray whiskers," said Freddie, "like a real grandfather."

All around the old one were baboons of varying sizes. A mother held a tiny baby in her arms. Six or eight young animals chased each other around the log. Others were climbing up and down the drooping branches of the trees.

"They're so funny," said Flossie. "I wish we had some in our back yard."

While everyone else took photographs, Jim wrote in his notebook. Then they drove deeper into the forest. Soon they stopped to watch a rhinoceros moving quietly among the trees.

Farther on, Nan spotted elephants across a meadow. Richard drove closer.

"Can we go right up to them, please?" Nan asked.

"No, sorry," Richard said. "If they should charge they could overturn the landrover."

"Elephants are often nervous," Billy added. "It's best to leave them alone."

A short time later the car drove out of the woods onto the shore of Lake Manyara.

"Wow! It's huge!" exclaimed Bert.

"Oh, look at the big birds!" said Flossie.

Swimming in the shallow water were half a dozen plump white storks with long red beaks.

"Pelicans, too," said Nan, pointing to a log. Three gray birds with large pouches stood in a row solemnly watching the travelers.

"You can get out here for a while," said Richard as he parked beneath a tree. "It's safe at this time of day. The big animals don't come around."

"Great!" said Bert. "I want to look for signs of the poachers."

"And maybe we'll meet Simba Sam," Freddie spoke up. "He said he was here at the lake!"

While the Bartons took notes on the birds and photographed them, the others scoured the shore for clues.

Nan, Freddie, and Richard went one way. Bert, Flossie, and Billy walked in the opposite direction.

Suddenly Bert and his companions heard shrill cries in the forest to their right.

"Those are baboons," Billy explained.

Moments later several of the animals burst from the trees and raced along the ground on all fours. Behind them came others with tiny babies clinging to their backs. More swung through the branches, crying loudly.

"Something has frightened them," said Billy. "Let's see if we can find out what happened."

He signaled for silence and slipped in among the trees. Flossie went next, followed by Bert. They moved along quietly, pushing through vines and ducking low, leafy branches. Suddenly they heard deep voices behind a thick growth of brush.

Cautiously they peeked around it into an open grassy place.

"Oh!" exclaimed Flossie, and clapped her hand over her mouth. Four rough-looking men were picking up limp baboons from the ground and putting them onto the floor of a zebra bus. The tallest man had a straggly blond beard. Slung over his shoulder on a strap was a weapon that looked like a gun.

At Flossie's exclamation, the men looked up. For an instant they froze. Then the bearded one snapped, "Grab 'em!"

The children turned and ran as fast as they could.

"Help!" screamed Flossie as she raced along,

For an instant, the men froze.

holding her brother's hand. Bursting out on the shore, the trio dashed to the landrover, yelling. But by the time they reached Jim and Tippy, the poachers had ducked back into the forest.

Breathlessly Bert told what had happened.

"I know that clearing," said Richard. "Everybody into the car. We must check on the animals! Boys, radio the rangers at the park gate to be on the lookout for a zebra bus with four men in it!"

Bert and Billy flashed the message just before the landrover reached the grassy place. The zebra bus and the poachers were gone.

"Look!" said Nan. "There's one of the baboons!"

A large animal with long grayish-brown fur lay on the ground as if in a daze.

"It's been shot with a sedative," said Billy. "We'll take it to the hotel."

"Okay," Richard said. "When it comes around, one of the rangers can bring it back here."

Quickly the girls moved the camera equipment, and Bert and Freddie placed the limp body on the seat beside Tippy. Billy radioed the gate again. No zebra bus had gone through in the last twenty minutes.

"Is there another way out of here?" Bert asked.

"Yes," Billy replied. "The poachers may not have used the park trails." He pointed to the left. "If they keep going through the forest that way, they'll hit the main road sooner or later."

"Now we know who stole the bus from the hotel," Bert said.

While they talked, he had been examining the ground. "See?" he said. "Here are their tire marks. Maybe we could follow them."

"We'll try," said Richard. "Everybody aboard."

A few minutes later they were driving slowly through the forest following the tracks. The young detectives kept sharp watch for signs of the fleeing men.

Suddenly Bert called softly for Richard to stop.

"Shhh!" said Nan, seeing what her twin had spotted. Amid the thick brush ahead were the stripes of the bus!

Richard brought the landrover to a quiet halt and everyone listened intently. Gruff voices were heard, talking angrily.

Bert stood up and looked through the open top. "They're stuck in a ditch!" he whispered.

"Good! Now we've got them," said Richard. "Jim and I will get out and cover them with rifles. Bert, you and Billy radio the rangers!"

But before anyone could move, a huge gray elephant stepped from among the trees and stood in front of the car!

"He—he's immense," Nan gasped.

Silently, two more of the big beasts appeared

from either side. Standing close to the landrover, they pulled bark from the trees and ate
it.

"What'll we do?" Freddie quavered.

"Sh-h," Billy said.

Suddenly one of the animals bumped against
the car. Then a long trunk came through the
opening in the top and waved around their
heads!

CHAPTER VIII

A WILD CHASE

"DON'T move," whispered Richard.

They all waited, still as mice, while the elephant's trunk explored the inside of the car. Then it withdrew. For a long time the big beasts fed from the trees around the landrover. Finally they moved on into the forest.

"Whew!" said Freddie. "Am I glad they're gone!"

"Yes. But so are the poachers," Bert muttered. He pointed toward the brush. The zebra bus had disappeared.

"What luck!" Richard said grimly. "Well, let's follow their tracks. We might still be able to catch them."

They drove a fair distance through the forest, until they came to the main road. Here the tracks ended.

Disappointed, Jim said, "We might as well go back to the hotel. The baboon may regain consciousness soon."

Everyone was silent on the return trip. Then all at once Richard stopped the car. "There's a sight you must see," he said.

Stretched out along a heavy limb in a large tree was a dozing lion!

"I never heard of lions climbing trees!" Nan exclaimed.

"They don't usually," Tippy said, readying her camera. "But these lions at Lake Manyara do. They like to lie on the branches."

"Why?" asked Nan.

"Some people think it's to escape the flies," Billy replied. "Others say it is so they can see over the tall grass while watching for game."

When they reached the gate, a ranger in a green uniform stepped from the gatehouse to report that the poachers had not been picked up, but the zebra bus had been discovered a few minutes earlier.

"It was empty," he said. "Ten miles from here in a field. The gang must have transferred the baboons to another car."

Richard nodded. "We almost caught them, except that a bunch of elephants played a trick on us!"

Just before they reached the lodge, the radio crackled and pipe music was heard.

"Simba Sam here," said the now familiar voice. "I'm on my way to Ngorongoro Crater. And I think You-Know-Who is going there, too. I'm hurrying to catch up."

"Who are you looking for, Simba Sam?" asked Bert.

But instead of an answer, there came more pipe music. Although the children called his name several times, Simba Sam did not speak again.

Freddie said, "I'll bet while he was looking for the poachers he discovered we were doing the same thing."

"Maybe he'll rescue Billy's uncle from the gang before we get a chance," put in Flossie.

"Now, Flossie," said Bert, "you know we can't be certain they kidnapped Bob Buyanda."

"No," Billy said. "But it's the only good explanation of why he disappeared. What do you think, Dad?"

"I think it's best not to jump to conclusions," Richard replied firmly.

"Well, Simba Sam didn't teach us any Swahili this time," Freddie said. "How about you, Billy?"

The boy smiled. "Sure. What do you want to know?"

"How do you say boat?"

"*Mashua.*"

"Tonight," Nan suggested.

"Jioni."

"Nice," said Flossie.

"Zuri."

The minutes flew by and soon the landrover passed the front garden and stopped at the hotel door. There the sleeping baboon was turned over to attendants, who took it to a large cage where it could recover in safety.

Before the travelers could enter the building, the hotel manager came running out. He spoke excitedly to Richard in Swahili. The twins caught only one word—Twiga.

"Billy, what is he saying?" Bert asked.

"Crackers is in the lobby! Come on!"

Dashing inside, the children saw a number of guests laughing at an odd sight. The giraffe stood in front of the registration desk, looking solemnly at the clerk.

The Bobbseys joined in the laughter. "I think Crackers wants a room," Nan said.

"We'll have to get her out of here," Billy declared.

As the hotel manager and Jim came in, the children quietly walked up to the giraffe.

"Do you have any crackers, Floss?" Nan asked.

"Yes." The little girl brought a small package out of her pocket and held up one of the crackers. Twiga turned and looked at her with great soft eyes, then bent her head and gently took the tidbit.

"Come along now," said Flossie and walked

"I think Crackers wants a room," Nan said.

slowly toward the terrace door. The giraffe followed, taking another cracker from Flossie's hand. The other children tiptoed silently along while the guests watched, curious and smiling.

"Lead her straight across the terrace around to the drivers' quarters in the back," Bert said.

An unpleasant surprise awaited them outside the door. Danny Rugg was leaning against a wall, obviously bored. When he saw them, he threw a stone and hit Crackers in the side. The giraffe shied and dashed off toward the swimming pool!

"Stop!" cried Nan and Flossie. "Bert, Billy, catch her!"

The twins raced after the giraffe, with the Bartons, the Buyandas, and a number of hotel guests behind them.

Startled sunbathers screamed and jumped into the water as Crackers galloped around the pool.

For a few moments the air was filled with frantic yells and shouted instructions, until Bert and Billy managed to head Crackers off on the other side of the terrace.

They threw their arms around her, and Nan spoke soothingly as they steered the giraffe back to her shed.

When Bert closed the door, he noticed that the padlock had been pried loose.

"I bet it was Danny!" Bert said. "He probably wanted to get back at us for this morning."

"I'll fix this lock," Richard said, "and we'll keep an eye on the shed until we leave." He added that he wanted everyone to be ready to travel after lunch.

The ride in the afternoon took hours. They passed herds of zebra, buffalo, and antelope grazing together. Tippy took a number of photographs while Jim wrote in his notebook.

"I like gnus," Freddie said as they passed two of the hump-shouldered animals. "They have such long, funny faces."

"You should call them wildebeest," Billy told him. "That's their African name."

At last the landrover wound up a very steep road. Tall, thin trees with drooping gray moss grew on the sheer slope above and below them.

"This is the outside of Ngorongoro Crater," said Billy.

At the top they stopped in a small parking lot to look down inside the crater.

The twins caught their breath. "Oh-h, it's so big!" whispered Flossie.

Far below lay a vast floor of pale green grass and trees. "It's so huge you can't even see the other side," said Bert.

"Tomorrow we'll ride down into it," said Richard. "But now we'll go to the Crater Inn and spend the night."

They drove on and soon turned into a stone gateway. Richard pulled up in front of a long, low building with a high-peaked roof.

"Oh, look! More storks!" Nan said as she climbed out of the car. Several large birds with long bills were walking slowly past the hotel.

"They're pretty tame," Billy said.

"Can we play with them?" Freddie asked.

"After supper, maybe," Tippy said. "But you have to be careful."

An hour later the twins met in the dining room for a delicious dinner of roast beef, potatoes and a special African vegetable. For dessert there was ice cream.

"Boy, am I stuffed," Freddie declared when he was finished.

"Billy said he would be in the summerhouse after supper," Bert announced. "Come on, let's join him." The twins walked next door into a small building where their friend was already looking through a telescope at the green fields below.

The children took turns with the instrument, and Freddie spied a stork walking solemnly along the lawn.

"I'm going to follow him." he said.

"Okay, I'll come with you," Billy offered. The two slipped outside just as the bird rounded the inn. He started toward some heavy brush growing at the far end of the grounds. Reaching it, he suddenly flew a short distance and landed out of sight.

"Too bad," Billy said. "We lost him."

Just then they heard an odd whistle. "That's

my Uncle Bob's signal again!" Billy exclaimed.

"It came from somewhere in those bushes," Freddie said.

"Right. I'm going to see who's doing it!" Billy declared. "You stay here, Freddie."

He slipped quietly into the thicket. Freddie waited, listening anxiously. Minutes ticked by. It was getting dark, and the trees and bushes looked like eerie monsters silhouetted against the dusky sky. Freddie became chilly and frightened.

"Billy!" he called out. "Billy, where are you? Come back, please!"

There was no answer.

CHAPTER IX

THE MASAI VILLAGE

"BILLY!"

Still no answer.

Scared, Freddie started to run back to the inn. Halfway there he met Richard and Jim hurrying toward him.

"Where were you?" asked Jim sternly. "It's almost dark. We were worried."

Freddie explained what had happened.

"Jim, why don't you wait here with Freddie? I'll go look for my son," Richard said. Jim nodded and Billy's father disappeared into the thicket.

"Billy!" he called out. "Where are you? Answer at once!"

"Here I am!" came Billy's voice faintly.

"Come back right away!" his father ordered.

Five minutes later the brush crackled and the two Africans stepped out.

"You had us worried," Richard scolded his son.

"I'm sorry. But I wanted to follow the person who was whistling. If you and Freddie hadn't called me, I might have caught him."

"Or you might have walked right into a trap!"

Back at the inn, they found Tippy, the girls, and Bert in the lounge before a large fireplace. Nearby was a glittering Christmas tree.

"I have something to say to everyone," Richard announced. "If you should hear that strange whistle, you must not try to catch the person. It's dangerous. Just tell me. I'll take care of it. You understand?"

They all promised, and Nan said, "By the way, we haven't seen Mr. Needles and Soper around."

"They're staying at a larger hotel called The Lodge. Your parents are there, too. We'll join them tomorrow night."

After a few minutes Richard and Billy said goodnight. "See you *kesho!*" Billy said.

"What's *kesho?*" Nan asked.

"Tomorrow!"

Half an hour later the travelers were in bed and the lights were out. Flossie spoke up. "Nan, Tippy?"

"Yes?" the two answered sleepily.

"I almost forgot. *Kesho* is Christmas Eve!"

Tippy chuckled. "It seems odd, doesn't it, not to have snow."

"And we still have some shopping to do, Floss," Nan added.

After breakfast next day Richard and Billy were waiting in the landrover in front of the inn.

"Where's Crackers?" asked Flossie as the twins piled in with cameras, sweaters, Bert's lariat, and box lunches packed by the hotel.

"She'll stay here for the day," Billy said. "We'll pick her up when we come back, then go on to The Lodge."

The motor roared and they were on their way. Eagerly the children looked out the open windows at the rolling green hills. Soon they turned down a steep, rutted road into the crater.

"Hang on, everybody!" shouted Richard as his passengers bounced on the seats.

When they reached the bottom, they drove toward a circle of huts surrounded by a thorn fence.

"This is our home village," said Richard.

"Now you'll meet my grandfather," added Billy. His eyes were bright with excitement.

The landrover came to a halt, and a crowd of men and boys wearing red cloth togas and carrying spears ran out to meet them.

Behind them appeared women and girls

dressed in long brown garments. Many had wide bead necklaces.

"Some of them have no hair!" whispered Flossie, surprised.

"It is the custom for old men, women, and children to shave their heads," Billy explained.

Amid excited greetings in Swahili, the Buyandas led the visitors through an opening in the fence into a yard of hard-packed mud.

"Wait here," Richard said.

He and Billy disappeared into one of the huts. Soon they returned with an old man. He was tall and straight as a spear.

His ear lobes had been pierced and stretched to make large openings. From the bottom dangled copper disks and from the top of each ear hung large beaded rings.

The Americans were introduced and the grandfather spoke to them with Billy as a translator. He gave Tippy and Jim permission to take pictures and make notes about the village.

"You may look around all you want," he told the children. He patted Billy's shoulder, "My grandson will be your host." Then the old man and Richard excused themselves and went inside the hut.

Billy led the twins over to a group of six children who had been watching curiously. He introduced them all.

"Jambo sana," said the twins.

The Masai children smiled to hear their

language spoken by the visitors. *"Jambo sana,"* they chorused.

At first they were shy, but soon the boys were showing Bert and Freddie how to throw the spears.

Billy explained that Masai boys often herded cattle. "We use the spears to fight off lions," he said.

In return, Bert demonstrated how to use a lasso, and told about American cowboys.

Meanwhile, the Masai girls showed the Bobbsey sisters their necklaces. "They're so pretty," exclaimed Flossie. "Red, blue, yellow, and white beads!"

"There are different kinds," said one very tall girl who spoke English. "The most elaborate ones are those we wear when we're married."

"I love the way the colors are in bands," said Nan.

Just then, Richard came out of his father's hut and called, "Time to go!"

Regretfully the children said good-by. The other twins left, but Nan lingered for a last look at the tall girl's necklace.

"I'm going to try to find one like that in the hotel gift shop," she thought as she hurried across the yard.

Suddenly she heard pipe music! It was the tune Simba Sam always played!

"It's coming from Grandfather Buyanda's

hut," she thought. "Maybe Simba Sam is a friend of his."

She ran over to the low doorway.

"Hello!" she called. The music stopped at once. Before she could call again she felt a hand on her shoulder. She turned around to see Richard.

"Come on, Nan," he said. "We're waiting for you."

"I think Simba Sam's in there," whispered Nan. "I heard his pipe!"

Richard frowned. "Anyone could be playing. People bring all kinds of musical instruments from Nairobi. But wait here, I'll take a look."

He walked into the hut and came out a few minutes later.

"You were mistaken. No one's in there besides my father, and he wasn't playing. Now come along. We have no time to waste."

Reluctantly Nan followed him to the landrover. For several hours they drove around taking pictures of more animals. The twins took turns looking at those far away with Jim's binoculars.

After a while Freddie became hungry. "Is it time for lunch yet?" he asked.

"Soon," Richard replied. "We're heading for a picnic area now."

He drove into a grove of tall trees with light yellow bark and long drooping branches.

"These are called fever trees," Billy said. He

explained that medicine was made from their bark to cure yellow fever.

They reached a large clearing. Richard parked at one side and the travelers scrambled out of the car. They sat down under a tree and ate fried chicken from their lunch boxes.

Suddenly a large monkey swung down out of the branches. Quicker than a wink, he snatched Bert's drumstick and ran away.

"Hey, that's mine!" cried Bert.

The monkey sat down a dozen feet away and ate the meat. More monkeys arrived and tried to take it away from him, but he scooted off.

Billy grinned. "Cut out the monkey business, will you, Bert?" he quipped.

Bert made a face. "Anyway, who cares? I have plenty more chicken."

After a short rest, the travelers drove on. They saw elephants, lions, wart hogs, vultures, and many other birds and beasts. Now and then they encountered tourists in zebra buses. But there was no sign of Needles or Soper anywhere. Nor was there any clue to the poachers.

Late in the afternoon the landrover drew up beside a huge lake with hundreds of bright pink flamingoes standing on its shore.

"They are bee-yoo-ti-ful!" exclaimed Flossie.

"Can you stop a minute, Richard?" Tippy asked. "I want to get some shots."

"Don't take too long," Richard warned. "We must head for the hotel soon. It looks like rain."

The children were so excited that they had not noticed the storm clouds.

"You're right, Dad," Billy said now. "We'd better get out of here fast."

"Why?" Bert asked. "We won't get wet."

"But the road turns to mud," Billy explained, "and we might be stuck down here all night."

He had hardly finished speaking when there was a streak of lightning. A rumble of thunder followed, and raindrops splattered against the windshield.

While the landrover sped toward the wall of the crater, the passengers lowered the roof and rolled up the windows. Soon they were climbing uphill. When they rounded the first curve, they saw a blue car with a flat tire parked on the side. A tall man jumped out and waved to them.

"It's Mr. Needles!" Nan exclaimed. "And he's alone."

Richard slowed down and Jim opened the door. "Get in," he said to Needles. "We have no time to lose."

The man climbed into the seat beside Tippy. "Thank you," he said, wiping the rain from his forehead with a handkerchief.

"Hold tight!" Richard said and gunned the motor. The landrover roared up the rough road, splattering mud on the windows.

Flossie borrowed Jim's binoculars to look at the storm-tossed trees below.

"Mr. Needles," Nan said, "where's your friend?"

"Hey, that's mine!" cried Bert.

"Back at The Lodge. Poor Soper's not feeling well."

The next moment Flossie squeezed her sister's hand and gave her the binoculars. They had just come around a long bend, and Needles' stranded car could be seen through the left side window.

"See those trees?" Flossie mumbled. "They'll be uprooted if the storm keeps up."

Trees were all Nan could see at first, but then she spotted the car.

Mr. Soper was crouched behind the wheel!

CHAPTER X

MERRY CHRISTMAS!

MR. NEEDLES had told a lie! His friend was not back at The Lodge. He was sitting in their car on the crater road!

Nan was about to put down the binoculars, when she noticed a tall Masai man standing behind a tree some distance from Soper. Heedless of the pouring rain, he was watching the disabled car. Nan had only a glimpse of his face before the landrover rounded another bend and the scene was lost.

Nan lowered the glasses and exchanged looks with Flossie. She put her finger on her lips and her younger sister nodded.

By the time they reached the top, the rain

had stopped. They drove to the inn, where they picked up the giraffe in her trailer, then continued to The Lodge. It was a large stone building, and Richard stopped in front. Mr. Needles jumped out.

"Thank you very much," he said with a crooked smile and quickly walked into the hotel. As soon as he had disappeared, Nan and Flossie told what they had seen through the binoculars.

"So Needles left Soper down in the crater," Jim said. "He'll be stuck there all night unless Needles goes down and picks him up later."

"But why would he stay there?" Flossie asked.

"I know," Bert said. "He was afraid that Nan would recognize him, and ask him for the package. It's too much of a risk for them."

Jim agreed. "That was a dumb thing for him to do in the first place, stealing Bob Buyanda's gift."

Nan was puzzled about the Masai man she had seen. "Maybe he's a ranger and will arrest Mr. Soper," she said.

"I doubt that," Richard said thoughtfully. "I don't think any of the special patrols are down there yet."

As they went into the hotel, Tippy said that the youngsters would have dinner with their parents. Afterwards everyone would meet the Buyandas in the main lounge to exchange Christmas gifts.

Billy grinned. "That'll be great!"

But his father shook his head. "I'm sorry but I promised to join the patrol in the crater tonight," he said. "I'll wish you Merry Christmas now and Billy will be Santa Claus for both of us."

Soon the travelers were in cozy, wood-paneled bedrooms on the floor below the lobby.

Freddie went to the sliding glass doors and exclaimed, "Wow! This whole wall is a window!"

He strained to look out into the evening. It was misty and almost dark by now.

"It's spooky out there," he said, and suddenly he gasped. "I see a big black thing, and it's coming this way!"

Bert glanced out. "What are you talking about? Nothing's there! Your imagination must be playing tricks on you." He pulled the cord and drew the heavy draperies together.

Jim patted the little boy on the shoulder. "You may have seen a Masai cow. They come around sometimes," he said. "Nothing to be afraid of."

Meanwhile, Nan and Flossie were hurrying into the brightly lighted gift shop in the lobby.

"Hey, look who's in there," Flossie whispered. "Mr. Needles!"

The girls pretended to examine the toy spears and shields in the window. Among them was a roaring wooden lion. Mr. Needles strolled over, picked it up, looked at the under-side, and set it down again. Then he walked out.

"Hello," said Nan. But he did not answer.

"He's not very nice," Flossie declared, and followed her sister into the shop.

Nan turned over the lion and glanced at the bottom. In red crayon was the number 12 and the word *jioni*—Swahili for *tonight!*

"This must be the go-ahead!" Nan whispered excitedly. "A lion with that word means all is ready!"

"May I help you?" the saleswoman asked.

"Yes," said Nan, putting back the carving. "We want a Masai necklace."

The woman showed them several, and they picked out a flat collar of bright red, blue, and yellow beads.

"That's for Tippy," Nan said. "Now let's select something for Mother and Dad and the others."

When they had finished their shopping, the sisters carried the boxes downstairs and told Tippy about Mr. Needles. Nan telephoned the boys to come in, and told them what had taken place in the shop.

"You're probably right about those lions," Bert said. "I wish we could have had a look at the other two."

Nan smiled. "How would you like your Christmas present right now?"

"Am I getting a lion?"

"I see a big black thing!" Freddie gasped.

"You'll find out." She ran to her suitcase and brought back the gaily wrapped package.

"Merry Christmas," she said. "Go ahead, open it!"

Bert did. He held up the carving with a big grin on his face. "Thank you, Nan. I like it for two reasons: First, it's beautiful, and second, I never got a clue for Christmas before!"

Carefully he examined the blurred red marks on the bottom. "That looks like a figure 8 and *jioni* after it," he declared. "What do you think?" The carving was passed around and everyone agreed.

"There must be a spy in each hotel," Nan said. "He finds out if the men are on guard and where they are patroling. Then he leaves a lion in the gift shop with the message on it."

"But what about the number?" Tippy asked.

"That must mean the area where they are to strike," Bert reasoned. "No doubt they have a code."

"And Needles and Soper check the carving and flash the green light," Jim added.

"But why," Bert said, "does the gang follow the route of the safaris, with all these people around?"

"I think I have the answer to that," Tippy replied. "The special patrols are based at the hotels. That means the spy can keep an eye on their movements and inform Needles."

"It looks like they are planning to strike tonight," Jim said. "Let me call Richard."

When he had spoken to the ranger, he said, "The patrol will be out full force. A friend of Richard's will watch for the green signal. When things begin to happen, we'll be alerted. Meanwhile, let's enjoy Christmas Eve!"

The children joined their parents for a delicious dinner of turkey and all the American trimmings. Although they watched for Needles and Soper, they did not see the two men.

Afterwards they carried their shopping bags into the lounge, where a tall tree was decorated with tinsel and colored balls. Billy was waiting with two long, narrow packages wrapped in red paper.

Other guests had gathered in a holiday spirit. One of them was an English clergyman, who offered to conduct a small service. After the Christmas story was read from scripture, the tourists broke into yuletide songs.

Among the guests were two Swiss, a Dutchman, a Swede, and a Scottish couple. They all knew the words and sang lustily.

"Oh, I just love Christmas," said Nan, and everyone began handing out presents. Gay paper and ribbons were scattered all over, and many thank-you's filled the room.

"A Masai shield," Freddie said excitedly as he unwrapped a big, brightly colored toy with circular designs. "Thank you, Bert, it's neat!"

Billy explained that the circles stood for bravery, and only a very bold warrior could put them on his shield.

From Bert and Freddie, Nan received a bracelet with dangling ivory elephants. Flossie got a small stone hippopotamus. Both girls were delighted.

"This is great!" said Billy as he tested a long, tubular flashlight. A card on it said, "From all the Bobbseys."

"And here's one for your father," Bert said. "So you can find your way around the crater at night."

Billy handed him a package. "This is for all of you from my father and me." He turned to Tippy. "Yours is the same," he said and gave her one, too.

Inside each was a black wood carving of a Masai man carrying a spear.

"Oh, it's beautiful!" Nan exclaimed, and all thanked the African boy warmly.

There were other gifts, too, including a carved wooden elephant which the twins had bought for their parents.

"And tomorrow we'll give Crackers something," Flossie declared.

As she spoke, a loud bell rang and the buzzing in the lobby quieted down.

"Ladies and gentlemen," the hotel manager announced, "we will now have a slide contest. Everyone who has taken a transparency of an animal may enter it. The best picture by an adult and the best picture by a child will receive a prize."

"We've snapped lots of pictures," Nan said, "but none of them have been developed."

"Mine are," Freddie spoke up. "Remember the slides I brought to show Jim?"

"But those aren't wild animals," Flossie objected.

"Just the same, they're animals. Nobody said they have to be wild! I'm going to enter one. Wait here, I'll get them."

"I'll come with you," Nan said. "I want to put on my sweater."

They got their room keys and went down the polished wooden steps and along the hall.

"I'll be out in a minute," Nan said, unlocking the girls' door.

"Hurry up," Freddie said. "It's creepy down here with no one around."

He walked into his room and took the box with the slides from his suitcase. Then he remembered that the huge, dark crater was just outside the window. A chill ran up and down his spine, but he could not resist peeking through the drapes. He pulled them apart just a little, then gave a sigh of relief. No strange creature was in sight!

All at once he gasped. His eyes popped and his heart skipped a beat. Far out in the crater a Roman candle shot red, green, and yellow balls high into the air!

"It's Fourth of July!" Freddie cried and dashed into the hall.

Nan came out of her room. "Fourth of July? What are you talking about?"

"Come here and see!"

They both ran to the big window and peered out. Another Roman candle shot into the sky.

"The poachers! They're signaling!" Nan said. "Come on, we'll give the alarm!"

By the time the children reached the lobby, everyone was watching the strange display of fireworks.

"Round up the patrols!" Freddie shouted. "The poachers are signaling again!"

Several guests turned to look at him, then the man from Sweden said, "Those aren't poachers! The Italians are coming!"

"The Italians?" Nan asked. "What do you mean?"

It was obvious that she and Freddie were the only ones who had not heard the news. A touring party from Rome was arriving one day early. Apparently some of them had brought along Christmas fireworks and were shooting Roman candles out of the bus.

Jim smiled. "They do that in Italy," he said, "on feast days."

Minutes later, with a lot of backfiring, a small bus pulled up in front of the hotel. Out piled a group of excited men, women, and children. Some of the youngsters carried Roman candles and skyrockets in their hands.

With big smiles and wishes of *Buon Natale* they streamed into the lobby.

The manager frowned and smiled alternately. "It's nice to have you with us," he said. "But you're a day early and we have no room! What are we going to do with all of you?"

A mustachioed man held out his hand and said in good English, "I don't know! The inn was filled up, too!"

Mr. Bobbsey spoke up. "I see you have a number of children here. Perhaps they could double up and room with ours."

"Hey, neat!" Freddie said and everyone agreed.

With nearly half of the overflow crowd being taken care of this way, the manager found that he had enough cots to put up the grownups. Now the hotel buzzed with excitement.

The chef, who was Italian, too, was so happy to see his fellow countrymen that he prepared a Christmas Eve snack, Roman style, and everyone enjoyed tasty meats and fresh fruits.

Suddenly the general hubbub was broken by a sharp cry from one corner of the lobby.

"Ow!" cried Danny Rugg. All eyes turned to see what had happened.

An Italian boy had punched Danny in the nose and snatched a skyrocket from the bully's hand!

CHAPTER XI

A JOKE ON DANNY

"FABRIZIO, *viene qui!*" the boy's father boomed. Fabrizio looked up and went over to his father. There was a voluble exchange of Italian words, and Fabrizio pointed to Danny, who, by this time, had bent over to retrieve the rocket.

Mr. Rugg walked up to Danny and said sternly, "Did you buy this from Fabrizio?"

Danny shook his head.

"Then give it back!" Mr. Rugg reached for the rocket, but Danny jerked it away. In doing so, it flew across the room, landing on a table beside an ashtray. In the tray was a smoldering cigarette.

"Oh, look out!" someone shouted.

The fuse of the rocket had touched the cigarette. There was a hissing sound as it began to sputter.

"Down, everyone!" Jim commanded.

The guests dropped to the floor. The fuse continued to hiss; then with a great *swoosh* the rocket began to fly around the room. It went through a lamp shade, knocked three balls off the Christmas tree, and, as if by a guidance system, flew out the front door and into the darkness.

Everyone picked himself up from the floor and Fabrizio clapped his hands.

"Bravo! Bravo!" he said, and the others laughed. All but Mr. Rugg. With a grim look at his son, he took him by the arm and led him out of the lounge in embarrassment.

The manager said, "Get ready now for the photography contest."

"Here are my colored slides," Freddie said to Bert. "Which one shall I enter?" He handed the box to his brother.

"I don't know," Bert replied. "Let me look them over." He sat on a sofa and held each frame to the light of a nearby lamp. A broad grin spread across his face.

"I've got an idea!" he said. He stood up and went over to the manager, who was seated beside the slide projector.

"Down, everyone!" Jim commanded.

"We would like to enter two pictures," Bert said.

"Okay. Which ones?"

"These."

"Just fill out the questions on this form."

Bert did and returned to the others.

"What are you up to?" Freddie asked curiously.

"Wait and see."

Show time was here now, and the newly arrived guests from Rome took seats along with the rest. Danny Rugg, who had come back without his father, sidled into the front row, looking neither left nor right.

"Winners will be chosen by the amount of applause their entries receive," the manager announced. The lights went out, and the large color picture of a leopard appeared on the screen.

For twenty minutes the guests enjoyed beautiful photographs of the animals in the national parks.

"Did you enter a picture?" Freddie asked Jim.

"No, but Tippy did. There it is now. It's Crackers in the Animal Nursery in Nairobi."

On the screen flashed the shot of the giraffe in a wire pen. A good-looking black man in a khaki ranger uniform was feeding her a tidbit. His teeth shone brilliantly under a thin mustache.

Nan gasped in surprise, and Billy whispered, "That's my Uncle Bob."

"He's the man I saw spying on Mr. Soper in the crater!" Nan whispered back.

"Are you sure?"

"Looks just like him. Except he wore Masai clothes instead of the uniform."

As the onlookers were applauding, Billy told Bert the news. Now the twins could hardly wait for the contest to end so they could speak to the grownups.

Finally the childrens' pictures were shown. After a few minutes, the manager said, "This slide was taken by Freddie Bobbsey, of the United States. It is an American lion!"

On the screen appeared Snoop, the Bobbseys' pet cat. She was standing on the snow-covered garage roof with her back arched.

Everyone laughed and applauded loudly. Except Danny Rugg. He booed.

"You are a very rude boy!" said a woman sitting in back of him. Danny ignored her.

"And now we have something special," the manager went on. "It is the same lion, taken with the same camera, but by another photographer: Danny Rugg, of the United States."

The bully's mouth dropped open in disbelief. Onto the screen came a snow-covered tree, standing on a slant. A few onlookers snickered.

"Where's the lion?" somebody asked.

Then someone else caught on. "In the left hand corner!"

And there it was. The tip of Snoop's tail could be seen at the very edge of the picture.

The audience roared with laughter.

"Hey, Danny," Bert called out, "is that the big one that got away?"

The bully's face turned red and he ran out of the room amid the laughter. The lights went on, and the prizes were awarded. Tippy and the man from Scotland were tied for first place. Each received a book of African photographs. Freddie won the children's contest—the prize was a set of small carved animals.

"They're just what I always wanted," he said happily.

Mr. Bobbsey patted his son on the shoulder. "Good work, Freddie. We'll celebrate with hot chocolate. How about it?"

He and Mrs. Bobbsey led the way to a large table across the lounge.

No sooner was everyone seated, when Nan told her story about recognizing Billy's Uncle Bob.

"If you're right," Tippy said, "then Bob Buyanda is not a prisoner of the gang. And maybe he never was!"

"But Nan may be wrong," Jim cautioned. "You know, Nan, you only had a very brief look at that man in the crater."

"And it was raining hard," Bert added.

"I know," Nan said. "But I'm *almost* sure."

The manager came over to their table as they were finishing their chocolate. "Let's see if we can get all these youngsters settled down for the night," he said. Since he spoke several languages, he could confer with everyone.

Bert asked if Fabrizio would share his bed, and the Italian boy readily agreed. Fabrizio had a younger brother, Pasquale, and it was decided that he should team up with Freddie.

But there were two more boys in the family. Where would they stay?

Jim offered to vacate his bed and sleep on a sofa in the lounge.

With cries of Merry Christmas and good night to their parents, the six boys trooped off to their room. Pietro and Sylvestro, the other two Italians, were seven and eight. None of them spoke English, but it did not matter.

They laughed and giggled and used sign language. First they figured out how they could all sleep comfortably. Bert had the answer. One boy would lie in one direction, and his bedmate in the other.

Then they all skinned out of their clothes and headed for the shower. There was plenty of confusion, until Freddie suggested they let the Italians go first, because they had had such a long and tiring day.

Once in their pajamas, they sat on the sides

of their beds, gesticulating. Then the Italians said *buona notte,* and everyone climbed between the sheets, like sardines in a can.

The girls in the adjoining room had settled down already. Nan did not know how long she had been asleep when she was awakened by a thumping sound. She glanced at her watch. It was two o'clock in the morning.

"I wonder what's happening," Nan thought, worried. The noise was coming from the boys' room. *Thud! Thump!* Then there was the sound of muffled voices.

Nan slipped out of her room, tiptoed down the hall, and put her hand on the knob. Gingerly she opened the boys' door.

Plop! A flying pillow hit her in the face. Nan fell over backwards!

CHAPTER XII

THE STONE SHIP

A dark-haired boy with large brown eyes poked his head out the door.

"*Scusi! Scusi!*" he said, and helped Nan to her feet.

"What's going on in here?" Nan called out.

A light went on. Bert emerged, with the others peering out from behind him.

"Only a pillow fight, Nan," he replied, "and I'm afraid your brother Freddie started it."

Freddie giggled, ran back and flopped on his bed. Pasquale followed, and tickled Freddie's feet.

Whack! A pillow hit Pasquale and white feathers spilled into the air.

"Now you've done it!" Nan said, just as Tippy joined the scene.

"Come on," she said. "Let's get this room straightened up." She helped pick up the feathers, made the beds, and tried to quiet down the excited youngsters.

"But why go to sleep?" Bert said. "The poachers will strike tonight, and we're waiting for Richard's friend to tell us about the signal!"

Tippy shook her head. "They must have changed their minds. It's after two already."

Bert was disappointed. "And we were so sure that this would be it!"

"Look," said Nan. "Get some sleep. If there is any action, we'll hear about it. Okay?"

"Okay." The boys went to bed and the girls left. The rest of the night was quiet.

Next morning the twins and the Bartons hurried to the drivers' quarters. Billy and his father were putting Crackers in her trailer.

"I can't understand why nothing happened," Richard said wearily. "Unless maybe the Italians with their fireworks upset the poachers' plans?"

Jim shrugged. "Something sure did. Anyway, I have a hunch the poachers will go to Serengeti today."

"So will we. How soon can you be ready?" Richard asked.

"In half an hour," Tippy replied.

The travelers, who had said good-by to Mr. and Mrs. Bobbsey earlier, were in front of the hotel even sooner. While the luggage was being loaded into the landrover, the twins gathered around the giraffe in her trailer. Flossie had bought a new package of crackers from the hotel and held one up for the giraffe to take.

"Merry Christmas!" she said. Then she gave the package to Freddie. "You feed her while I get the other present."

Freddie did, and Flossie pulled a large red ribbon from her bag.

"How do we put it on her?" Freddie asked.

"I'll tie it while she's eating," said Flossie.

But every time she attempted it, the little giraffe straightened up.

"I'll help you," Bert offered. He lifted Flossie to his shoulders. Now she was face-to-face with Twiga.

"Hold still, Crackers," she said gently and put the ribbon around the giraffe's neck. Carefully she tied a big bow.

"That looks great!" Nan said.

"No one could ever get her mixed up with any other giraffe," Tippy said with a laugh as she helped Flossie off Bert's shoulders.

Crackers tossed her head once or twice, then gazed quietly down at the children.

"She doesn't seem to mind having the ribbon on," Nan remarked.

"I'm afraid she's getting *too* tame," Richard said as they climbed into the landrover. "In a few days we'll be turning her loose in her home park. It would be too bad if she didn't want to stay there."

He started the motor. At that moment Needles came out of the hotel. He stopped short and stared hard as the landrover and trailer moved away.

Freddie chuckled. "I guess he never saw a giraffe with a Christmas bow before."

"Who has?" Bert asked with a grin.

From Ngorongoro Crater to the next lodge was a long ride over a huge, grassy plain. The sun tanned the children's faces and the hot wind whipped back their hair as the landrover roared past hundreds of wildebeest, zebra, buffalo, and antelope.

Suddenly Flossie spotted a dust cloud on the long road behind them. It grew larger and larger.

"A truck is coming!" she announced.

"He's moving along pretty fast," Bert said.

Richard pulled over to let the newcomer pass. But the speeding truck headed straight for them! The girls screamed.

"He's going to hit us!" shouted Bert.

Richard turned the wheel hard and the landrover swerved onto the rough ground beside the road. The truck roared past in a cloud of dust.

"He's going to hit us!" shouted Bert.

"Whew!" Richard said, wiping his brow. "That driver must be crazy!"

"We should report him to the authorities," Jim said angrily.

"The truck belongs to the Hotel Supply Company," Nan stated. "I saw the name on the side."

"That's surprising," Billy said. "Their drivers are usually very careful." He reminded the twins that there were no stores in the wilderness.

"All the supplies for the hotels must come from Nairobi," he explained.

Just then the radio crackled and the familiar pipe music was heard. "Merry Christmas!" came the deep voice of Simba Sam.

"Merry Christmas," the travelers replied.

"I'm in the Serengeti Plain," Simba Sam said.

"We'd like to meet you," Freddie spoke up. "Can we?"

Simba Sam did not comment on the boy's suggestion, but went on: "I'll have big news soon. Until then, *kwaheri*."

"He never answers our questions," said Nan, disappointed.

"I wonder what the big news will be," Freddie said.

It was near noon when they saw a hill of huge rocks in the middle of the plain. Great round boulders and tall blocks of stone were jumbled together in one long, high mound. Heavy brush and small trees sprouted out of the cracks and grew around the base.

"It looks like a ship," Freddie declared.

Nan agreed. "And the plain is the sea!"

"It's even got smoke coming out of the top," said Flossie. "See?" She pointed to a shimmering plume rising above the outcrop.

"I doubt that it's coming out of those rocks," Tippy said. "Maybe there's a grass fire in back of the hill."

"Or it might not even be smoke at all," Billy said. "When the air is very hot, it looks like that."

Half an hour later the landrover entered a winding driveway, passed another big hill of stone and stopped in a large yard. Here and there were small round houses with pointed roofs.

"Those are guest houses," Billy said. "They're concrete copies of the thatched huts many African tribes use."

His father and Jim stepped from the car and went into the one marked "Office." Soon they came out.

"Tonight we sleep there," said Jim. He pointed across the yard toward some thorn trees. Beyond them was a long row of green tents.

"Oh, goody," exclaimed Freddie, and the other children beamed.

"This is going to be fun," said Nan as she and Flossie entered their tent. In the first room stood two cots. Behind that was a small dressing room with a shower.

"It even has its own little front porch," Flossie said. "This is just like playing house."

The girls poured water from a pitcher into china basins and washed themselves. They had just put on fresh shorts and tops when Jim called them.

"Anybody hungry?"

"I am!" the girls chorused and went outside. They found the Bartons sitting on their porch. Bert and Freddie emerged just then from the tent next to Jim and Tippy.

"I could eat an elephant," Bert announced. "But there's just one thing I want to do before we have lunch."

"What's that?" Nan asked.

"See if there's a lion in the gift shop window!"

The two older twins went to check on the clue, and five minutes later met the others in the dining room.

"Any luck?" Jim asked.

Bert shook his head. "But it's early. Maybe the spy will put it in later."

When they had finished eating, the sky had clouded over and it began to rain hard. Two hours later it stopped and the young twins skipped off to visit the giraffe in her pen.

As Bert and Nan walked across the yard they noticed Mr. Needles some distance away. He was walking in the opposite direction and did not see them.

"Let's find out where he's going," Nan said.

"You bet!" The two followed the man to the driveway and around the rocky hill. They moved cautiously, slipping from one boulder to another.

For a short while they lost sight of their quarry. But a few minutes later they heard someone talking on the other side of a big boulder.

"No action tonight," said Mr. Needles.

"The men aren't going to like it," came another voice.

"Their spy must have put a lion in the gift shop after I looked for it," Bert said under his breath.

Needles' voice came again. "It can't be helped, Jones. We got the message. The patrol has been increased again. You and the others stay at the hideout, and if—"

Just then Nan slipped and let out a gasp.

"Somebody's spying on us!" Needles hissed.

CHAPTER XIII

KIDNAPPED!

THE children froze in fright.

"I'll bet it's those twins," Needles muttered.

"The noise came from behind that rock," Jones added. "Let's get our hands on 'em!"

"Quick, under that brush!" Bert whispered and pulled Nan along with him.

Heavy footsteps moved toward them. Then they stopped. "Wait," Needles said. "I've got a better idea."

"What?"

"Come on, I'll tell you on the way."

The men walked off. Bert and Nan crawled out of their hiding place and ran back to the hotel. They found Freddie, Flossie, and Billy in the garden and quickly told them what had happened.

Jim and Richard came out a few seconds later and were quickly filled in on the new event.

Billy said excitedly, "Now we have enough proof to have Needles and Soper arrested, right, Dad?"

"Whoa! Not so fast!" replied his father. "Our job is to find the leaders of the gang. I suggest we keep watching them and see what happens."

"That's right," Jim agreed. "Remember, the gang has a spy at the hotel, or at least it's very likely that they do. If they find out about the arrest, the other members will scatter and we'll never round them up."

"By the way," Richard said, "we have some news, too. We inquired about that truck that almost hit us. The manager said it did not come here."

"He said there is no delivery due for the next two days," Jim added.

"Then where did it go?" asked Freddie.

"Maybe to one of the other national parks?" Nan suggested.

"No. We radioed the others. None of them expects to get supplies until next week."

"Then there's something fishy about it," Bert declared.

Jim smiled. "One more mystery for the Bobbseys. But before you attempt to solve that, let's go for a ride. There are a few places I want to see for my report. Tippy'll stay here, though. She's busy sorting out film and notes."

Bouncing over the plain in the landrover, the children first passed a herd of buffalo. Then they saw a line of dainty gazelles springing away from them.

"Tommies," said Freddie.

"And there's a bunch of cheetahs!" Nan exclaimed. A number of big spotted cats raced by the car.

"They're very fast," Richard said.

Jim was taking notes and he asked Richard to slow down at certain places, where he studied the vegetation. Finally he glanced at the setting sun and said, "Time to go back. We'd better take the short way so we'll make it before dark."

Richard turned around and picked up speed. In a few minutes they had to slow down, however, before a stream of muddy water rushing through a wide gully.

"Looks pretty deep," Richard said.

"That's because of the rain," Jim remarked.

"Where's the bridge?" asked Freddie.

"There isn't any," Richard replied. "The landrover can go right through the water if it isn't too deep."

He backed the car up for a short distance. Quickly the passengers lowered the roof and rolled up the windows.

"Shut 'em tight," Billy said, "or else you're in for a mud bath."

"All right, everybody," Richard said, "Here we go!" He gunned the motor and the land-rover shot down the gully and hit the stream. The children shrieked with excitement as muddy water splashed over the windows, shutting out the light.

The next moment the car roared up the opposite bank and onto flat ground.

"That was fun!" cried Flossie. "I'd like to do it again."

Richard laughed. "Not tonight, little *bibi*!"

"*Bibi* is Swahili for lady," Billy explained with a grin.

They made good time from then on and pulled up to The Lodge just before dark. As the children piled out they saw their parents walking toward the dining room.

"Mommy, Daddy!" called the younger twins, and the Bobbseys greeted each other with hugs.

"We arrived ten minutes ago," said Mrs. Bobbsey. "Where's Tippy?"

Before the children could answer, a stout man with a bristly gray beard came out of the manager's office.

"What about the accident?" he asked anxiously. "Anybody hurt?"

"Was anyone hurt?" the manager asked anxiously.

"What accident?" Richard asked.

"A ranger came in a landrover and said that your car had been found overturned in a gully, and that the children were hurt. He took your wife to the place, Mr. Barton."

"My wife!" exclaimed Jim. "Where is she now?"

"She isn't back yet," the manager replied.

"What time was this?" Richard asked.

"About an hour after you had gone." The man pulled an envelope from his pocket. "The ranger left this for you, Mr. Barton."

Jim opened it and read the note aloud: *"If you want your wife back, tell the Bobbsey Twins to cut out the snooping!"*

"Oh!" exclaimed Nan. "Tippy's been kidnapped!"

"How awful!" said Mrs. Bobbsey.

Mr. Bobbsey had taken the note from Jim. "It's not signed," he said, "but there's a drawing of a leopard on the bottom."

"This ranger," Jim asked grimly. "What did he look like?"

"About medium-sized, young, with close-cropped hair," the manager said. "I meet a lot of the rangers, but I'd never seen this one before."

"He was no more a ranger than I am," Bert declared. "He was a member of the Leopard Gang!"

"We can't wait any longer now," Richard

said. "We must question Needles and Soper at once. They'll know where Tippy is."

"I'm sorry," the manager said. "They left shortly after you went out today."

"They're probably headed for Masai Mara," said Billy. "That's the next safari stop."

"Right," said the manager. "I'll radio the lodge there to hold the men if they arrive."

"Better give the hotel a description of them," Bert suggested. "Needles and Soper must know we're on their trail. My guess is that they will use assumed names."

"And maybe even disguises," Nan added.

"That's possible," the manager agreed. "I'll also alert all patrols and tourist buses to be on the lookout for Mrs. Barton and that fake ranger."

The four men went into the office, and Billy said, "I'd better check on Crackers." He hurried away.

"Oh, Mommy," Flossie cried, "are they going to find Tippy?"

Freddie's lip was trembling and there were tears in Nan's eyes, too.

"Don't worry," Mrs. Bobbsey said gently. "Lots of people will be searching for her. Come along now, I want all of you to eat some supper."

The children and their mother went to the dining room, but no one was very hungry. Afterward, they took soup and sandwiches to the men in the manager's office. They were gathered around a large table listening to the radio.

"We can't understand it," said Mr. Bobbsey. "Where could the gang have gone with her? The Serengeti plain is so flat and open, and patrols are riding all over it. Yet no one has spotted that landrover."

"It has disappeared like magic," the manager said gloomily.

Jim said nothing, but he looked very worried.

"The kidnapping must have been that 'better idea' that Needles mentioned to the man he called Jones," Nan said.

Richard spoke up. "Mrs. Bobbsey, you and the children might as well go to bed. We'll wake you if there's any news."

In the morning the Bobbseys met Jim at breakfast. He looked pale and tired. There had been no word of Tippy.

"The Buyandas and I are going out to search in the landrover," he said.

"May we come?" Nan asked. "The more people looking for Tippy, the better."

"Okay," Jim agreed. "You do have sharp eyes."

"Mother and I are taking a trip in our tour bus this morning," said Mr. Bobbsey. "We'll be watching for her, too."

Shortly after breakfast the big car roared out of the yard with Richard at the wheel. The hotel manager had supplied box lunches and extra binoculars. For two hours the search party scoured the flat land with their powerful glasses. But they saw only animals and now and then a tourist bus.

Around noon Richard parked at the edge of a low bluff. They could see for miles across the grassy plain.

"We'll eat here," he announced, "and watch at the same time."

Despite their worry, the children ate their sandwiches and drank milk from a Thermos.

"Look, Jim!" exclaimed Billy suddenly. "I think I see tire tracks in the grass at the foot of the bluff."

Jim raised the binoculars to his eyes. "Right! Let's go down and examine them!"

"Someone must stay here at the radio," Richard said.

"We'll do that," the Bobbseys offered.

The two men, carrying rifles, and Billy stepped out of the car and disappeared down the bluff.

For a few minutes the twins quietly used the binoculars. Suddenly the radio sputtered. "Simba Sam here!" The familiar voice sounded excited. "I've found Tippy!"

CHAPTER XIV

WHISTLING CLUES

SAM'S voice seemed to flutter. "I'm in the—"
g-whee-whee-eeyowee—

"Something's happened to his radio!" Bert
said tensely.

The whistling screams continued. A minute
later, Sam's voice came through weakly.

"Mashua! Mashua!"

He gave a sudden sharp cry, then the radio
went silent.

"Sam!" cried Nan. "Simba Sam, where are
you?"

"What's the trouble?" Bert pressed.

The radio remained silent.

"The bad men caught him!" Flossie exclaimed.

"It may be." Bert frowned. He called out to Jim and the Buyandas. In a few minutes they scrambled over the edge of the bluff and hurried back to the car.

"What's up?" Richard asked.

Bert told what had happened.

"What about Tippy?" Jim asked eagerly. "Did you hear her voice?"

"No."

"But where are they?" Jim went on. "Didn't he give you any directions?"

"Nothing. Only the word *mashua*. And that means boat."

"But there's no water around here," Nan spoke up. "Unless he means Lake Manyara."

"There are other lakes," Richard said thoughtfully.

"The Indian Ocean isn't that far off either," Jim added. "Remember, we're on the east coast of Africa. It's only about an hour by plane from here to the shore."

"I just thought of something," Freddie said. "We heard a funny noise while Simba Sam was talking."

"Like what?"

"It was a sort of whistle and screams all at the same time," Flossie explained.

"Could have been static," Richard said. He picked up the microphone. "I'll radio ranger headquarters. Then we'll follow the tire tracks we found. They might lead us to Simba Sam and Tippy."

Soon the landrover was on its way. It was hard to make out the tracks and they had to go slowly.

"They look like marks made by a truck," Bert said.

"Right," Billy agreed. "And usually the trucks around here have business in the hotels or small settlements and stick to the roads. The fact that this one was out in the grassland suggests some funny business."

"Like poaching," Nan said.

"Maybe it's the truck that nearly hit us!" Bert said. "It would be perfect for the poachers. They could carry camping equipment or even sleep in it."

Richard nodded. "The rangers have been on the lookout for strange cars or vans," he said. "But no one would stop the Hotel Supply drivers. The company is well known around here."

"I wonder if any of their trucks are missing," Billy spoke up. "I'll radio the police in Nairobi and find out."

The others listened as he talked with headquarters. He was told that two trucks had been stolen from the supply firm the month before.

"That figures," Bert said excitedly. "But why do the poachers need two trucks?"

"They might use one for hunting and the other one to transport the stolen animals to wherever they sell them," Richard said.

Richard stopped the landrover.

"What's the matter?" Nan asked.

"See this? We've come to a road. And the tracks stop right here!" His voice was grim.

"Not again!" Bert exclaimed. "This is the second time we've lost the trail that way. Now what'll we do?"

"Go back to The Lodge," Jim said.

The searchers reached the hotel early in the afternoon and reported at once to the manager's office. Maps were spread out over the big table, and two rangers were studying them. One, a tall, bony man with keen black eyes, questioned the children about the radio message.

"We are checking the maps for streams and lakes in this area," he said.

Bert and Billy offered to help.

"Good," the man said. "We can use two more pairs of eyes."

"Crackers has to be fed," Billy said. "Flossie and Freddie, would you do it for me?"

"Sure," the younger twins promised.

"That long, one-story building next to the cage is the laundry. The men there will give you water. Nearby are some acacia trees. You can pick some nice leafy boughs. Crackers likes those."

Freddie and Flossie left the office and went over to the pen.

"Hello, Crackers," said Flossie as the giraffe walked over to the wire fence to see them. "I have a treat for you."

While Freddie took the bucket from the cage and went next door, Flossie fed the giraffe some crackers.

"I wish we could take you home with us," the little girl went on. "But you'll be much better off here in your own land."

The giraffe stared at her solemnly, then took another cracker.

When Freddie had put food and water in the pen, the twins made sure the door was securely latched. Then they started back toward the tents.

They rounded the corner of the laundry and noticed Danny Rugg kneeling on the ground. He was lining up small stones in front of him.

"What are you doing, Danny?" Freddie asked.

"Having target practice, silly!" Danny pointed to the huge rock outcrop a short distance away. "I'm going to pop off a couple of those funny animals."

The Bobbseys saw several little bright-eyed creatures sitting on top of the largest rock. Here and there other small heads with twitching whiskers peeped out from cracks.

"They almost look like groundhogs," Freddie thought. "Only much smaller."

"Don't throw stones at them," Flossie said. "You might hurt one."

"What do I care?" Danny retorted. He picked up a stone and hurled it.

The animals gave high whistling screams and darted out of sight.

Flossie excitedly grabbed Freddie's arm. "That noise!" she whispered. "It's the same sound we heard on the radio when Simba Sam was talking!"

As she spoke, a husky man with kinky black hair strode out of the laundry.

"That's enough!" he said sternly to Danny. "Now you get out of here and stop bothering the hyraxes."

Danny dropped the stone he was holding and raced off.

"What did you call those animals?" Freddie asked the man.

"They're rock hyraxes," he replied.

"Do they always live in these big piles of stone?" Flossie asked.

The man nodded. "Their homes are often in the outcrops."

The young twins waved to him and hurried away. "I'll bet Tippy and Sam are prisoners in one of those rock hills on the plain," said Freddie. "Remember the one that looked so much like a boat?"

"Don't throw stones at them," Flossie said.

"You're right!" Flossie said. "Maybe that's what Simba Sam meant when he said they were in a *mashua!*"

They dashed into the manager's office. "We know where Tippy and Simba Sam are!" Flossie cried.

The men and boys looked up from the maps in surprise, while the two told of their idea.

"That's pretty far-fetched," the tall ranger said. "It's much more likely the hideout is on a real boat somewhere near Mombasa or Dar- Es-Salaam. Those are cities where the gang could sell stolen animals or hides and horns."

"We've radioed Nairobi for an airplane," said the second ranger. "We're going to fly to the coastal area and search there."

"Police planes will be on the job, too," Richard said.

"All the same," Jim declared, "I think we should check out the children's theory."

Richard agreed. "We'll go right now."

The twins ran to get their flashlights, and Bert picked up his lariat. "Never know when you may need it," he said to himself.

"We should be back by the time the plane gets here," Richard said as he started the land-rover. Half an hour later the big outcrop appeared far ahead.

"It certainly does look like a boat," Nan remarked as they drew closer. In the waning daylight Richard pulled off the road and drove up to the huge rock pile. He parked at the base behind some heavy bushes.

"Now we must be very careful," he said quietly. "If this is the right place, some of the gang could be around. Also, there's danger from wild animals."

"How should we approach?" Bert asked. He tried to sound cool, but a chill ran up and down his spine.

"Jim, Billy, and I will station ourselves around the outside with rifles. The rest of you circle the place and look for an entrance. Everything clear?"

"Okay."

"And if you run into trouble, yell," Billy added.

Freddie and Flossie started to the right, while Bert and Nan walked quietly to the left.

"Plenty of hyraxes," Bert whispered. The beady-eyed creatures watched them from the rocks above.

"I hope we don't scare them," Nan said. "If they take off suddenly it might alert the crooks."

Nan spotted a broken place in some high brush at the base of the "boat." She and Bert quietly slipped into it. They faced a large split between two huge rocks.

"This looks as if it might lead somewhere," Bert said in a low voice.

"Should we call the others?" Nan wondered.

"Not yet. First let's make sure it's not a dead end."

"Don't flash your light," Nan whispered.

Bert nodded. Cautiously they walked into the darkness. Suddenly Bert's shin hit against something and he tripped. Then a grinding noise sounded above them.

A huge stone crashed down, blocking the way out!

CHAPTER XV

BOAT RESCUE

"WHAT happened?" Nan whispered.

"I tripped." Bert flashed his light on the floor of the narrow passage. There lay a rope. One end was tied around the stone slab that blocked the entrance. The other had been threaded through an iron ring imbedded low in one rocky wall. The rope was stretched across and tied to a ring on the opposite side.

"The stone was probably balanced up there," Nan said, aiming her light at a ledge above their heads.

"And when my leg hit the rope, it pulled the rock down," Bert added. "Now I'm sure we're in the gang's hideout. Who else would rig up a trap like this?"

"But how are we going to get out again?" Nan asked. She played her beam over the slab. It was wedged in tightly. "We'd better yell for help, Bert."

All at once a faint voice came from somewhere in the darkness.

"This is QQSM. Do you read me? Please answer. This is QQSM. Do you read me?"

"It sounds like Simba Sam!" Nan exclaimed. "Let's call him."

"No, don't. What if the crooks hear us? Besides, I'm beginning to wonder if Simba Sam is on our side after all. Maybe he lured us into this trap because he's in cahoots with the poachers!"

"I just can't believe that," Nan objected.

"But we have no proof whatever that Simba Sam's a good guy," Bert said. "Let's just walk down here carefully."

The two moved along the stone passage. The voice became louder, and it sounded tense.

Rounding a bend, Bert and Nan faced a stone wall.

"This is QQSM," said the familiar voice. "Can you hear me?"

"But no one's here!" Nan said, puzzled.

Bert flashed his light. They noticed a low, wide opening at the bottom of the wall.

"He must be on the other side," Bert said.

"Call him," Nan urged.

"No. Let's wriggle through and take a look for ourselves."

The children lay face down on the floor and turned off their lights. Side by side, they inched their way through the hole until they could see into a dimly lighted rock chamber. A man was kneeling on the other side with his back to them.

"QQSM here. Do you read me?" His voice sounded troubled.

"Simba Sam!" Nan blurted out. "We're here! The Bobbsey Twins!"

The man gasped and whirled around. He was the Masai whose picture they had seen during the contest on Christmas Eve. The man who had been feeding Crackers!

"You're Bob Buyanda!" Bert declared.

The detective was stunned for a moment, then he walked across the room and helped the children out of the hole.

"Now you know my secret," he said. "Yes, I'm Bob. And you must be Bert and Nan. How did you find me?"

Quickly they told all that had happened since Tippy was kidnapped. Then Bert asked, "How did you get caught?"

Buyanda grinned wryly. "I know what you're thinking. The great government agent and ranger outwitted by poachers."

"You're Bob Buyanda!" Bert declared.

Bert was embarrassed. "Well, I never thought they could capture you."

"They did it by trickery," Bob said. "I was shot with an anesthetic dart and passed out."

"How awful!" Nan declared.

"They are a tough bunch," Bob agreed. "But we'll get them! I'm sure none of them is here now, but we'll catch up with them."

"Mr. Buyanda," Nan said anxiously, "where's Tippy?"

"Call me Bob," the detective said with a smile, then answered the question. "I don't know exactly. She's in another room somewhere in this rock pile. Here, listen!" He took a deep breath and called out, "Tippy!"

"Yes!" the girl's voice was faint.

"Bert and I are here," Nan called.

"Are you prisoners, too?" their friend asked.

"Yes, but don't worry," Bert yelled. "We'll find a way out."

"But how?" Nan asked quietly. "Jim, Richard, and Billy are outside with Freddie and Flossie, but they don't know where we are."

"I tried to get help with my radio," Bob said. "But it must be broken. I couldn't raise anyone."

"Talking about the radio," Bert said, "why did you do that Simba Sam routine?"

"I'll tell you later. First, let's find a way out of here."

They looked around the chamber. Bert

noted cartons, canned goods, a pile of wood, and the remnants of a fire. Glancing at the ceiling, he saw a long, narrow passage slanting upwards through the rocks. At the end was a patch of blue sky.

"Maybe we could send a signal up that chimney," Bert suggested. "Remember, Nan, Freddie saw smoke coming from it before?"

"I thought of that," Bob said. "But so did the poachers. They took all the matches with them, including mine. Only left the radio. No doubt they broke it after they caught me."

"We heard you broadcast that you were in the *mashua*," Nan said.

"Good thing you did. You see, after I staked out this place and realized Tippy was in here, I called you. The next moment I was hit with the anesthetic dart. When I woke up, I found myself in this chamber."

"But how did the crooks get you down here?" Bert asked.

The detective pointed to a narrow passage at the other side of the rock chamber. "Through there, I guess. A wooden door is at the end of it."

Looking around for another way to attract attention, Nan saw a pair of small bright eyes peeking from a crack in the wall. Then a furry animal popped out and scampered across the floor.

"A hyrax!" Nan exclaimed.

"Yes," Bob said with a smile. "They've been keeping me company. There are lots of them up in that chimney."

Suddenly Nan had an idea. "Maybe the hyraxes can tell them where we are."

"What do you mean?" Bert asked.

"Let's scare them out of the chimney. They'll make that whistling scream as they run up into the daylight."

"That's a great idea!" Bob said. "There's a good chance my brother will hear them and come to investigate."

He stooped down. "Bert, you climb up on my shoulders, so you can reach the hole in the roof. Nan, hand him a piece of that firewood."

"I get it," said Bert, taking the wood. "You want me to beat this on the inside of the chimney."

"Right," said Bob. "At the same time, we'll all yell as loudly as we can. One, two, three—go!"

The prisoners shouted over and over while Bert whacked the wood against the stone. Whistling in fright, dozens of hyraxes scampered out of nooks and crannies in the narrow chimney and raced to the surface.

"Look at them go!" exclaimed Nan, watching the noisy animals dashing up the slanting passage into daylight.

The trio yelled until they were hoarse and all the hyraxes were gone.

Suddenly there came a shout from above. Billy peered down.

"Uncle Bob!" he cried. "Bert, Nan! How did you get in there?"

Bert explained. Then Bob told his nephew to look for the entrance. Billy called instructions to Jim and Richard.

"And keep an eye out for Tippy," Nan reminded him.

"Will do," Billy said and disappeared.

Soon the prisoners could hear distant pounding.

"Let's go," said Bob. "They're knocking the padlock off the door." He picked up a wooden pipe from the floor and put it in his pocket.

"I almost forgot my musical instrument," he said. "It's just a toy I bought in Nairobi. I figured it would be fun to add music to my Simba Sam act."

Then he lifted a package which was beside the radio. "Here's the gift I left for you at the hotel," he said, handing it to Bert. "You can open it later."

While Jim and the Buyandas were working on the padlock, Freddie and Flossie were climbing over the outcrop, calling through clefts and holes for Tippy.

Near the top of the great pile Freddie sat down to rest. The setting sun was hot and his round face was pink with exertion.

"Poor Tippy," said Flossie as she plopped

down next to him. "Where can she possibly be?"

"I'm here!" Tippy's voice came clearly. "Right here, Flossie!"

The twins looked around bewildered. "Where?" they chorused.

"Down in the rocks. I'm looking up through a round hole, but it's too high for me to climb out."

Freddie and Flossie stood up and searched excitedly for an opening among the rocks.

"I can see some leaves," said Tippy.

The twins glanced around and noticed a small tree growing out of a crevice. Quickly they clambered over to it. Flossie was first. She lifted the drooping branches.

"Here's the hole," she cried. Stepping closer, she slipped.

"Help!" she screeched and dropped out of sight!

CHAPTER XVI

DANNY GETS THE POINT

FREDDIE scrambled over to the hole and peered into it. Flossie was stuck in the narrow chimney looking up at him.

"Help!" she cried, waving her arms wildly.

Freddie reached down and grabbed his sister's hands, but hard as he tried, he could not pull her free.

"Tippy!" he called into the hole. "Can you push her up?"

"No," came the girl's muffled voice. "I can't reach her feet."

Freddie hurried to the edge of the rocks and shouted to the others. Bert climbed over the hill and raced toward him.

"What's the matter?" he asked.

"Flossie's stuck!"

Freddie led Bert to the hole. Looking down, Bert saw Flossie's face, red and wet with tears.

"Take it easy, Floss," Bert said. "We'll get you out in no time."

He grasped her wrists. Then, as he stood up, he pulled her free and set her on her feet.

"Thank you." Flossie gasped, and hugged him hard.

"Now we have to rescue Tippy," said Freddie. "She's down there in that hole!"

Just then the rest of the party arrived at the hilltop. Jim hurried to the hole and looked into it. His face lighted with relief.

"Tippy!" he called. "Where's the entrance?"

"The poachers let me down from the top on a rope," Tippy replied.

"Then that's how we'll have to get you out," said Bert. He took the lariat from his belt, made a loop in one end and tossed it to the prisoner.

"Slip it under your arms," he instructed. When Tippy was ready, the men pulled hard on the other end.

Soon Tippy's red hair appeared at the top of the hole and Jim reached out to help her.

"Oh, we're so glad you're safe!" Nan cried.

As the Bartons hugged each other, excited questions filled the air. The young twins were introduced to Bob Buyanda. Tippy shook the hand of the detective and smiled. "Thank goodness you're here!" she said. "Did they kidnap you, too?"

"We'll talk later," Richard interrupted. "It'll be dark soon. We must get back to The Lodge."

Bob agreed. "I wonder if my landrover is still where I left it," he said, and led the way to the bottom of the hill. Under some heavy over-hanging brush stood an old car.

The detective swung into the driver's seat and started the engine.

"It's all right," he said. "I guess the poach-ers didn't find it."

The sun was nearly gone as the two cars headed for the road. On the way, Billy radioed news of the double rescue to ranger head-quarters and the hotel. Then Bert and Nan told how they had found the missing detective.

When they arrived at The Lodge, the mana-ger invited everyone into his office where Mr. and Mrs. Bobbsey were waiting. They were all in high spirits when they went into the dining room, where a large round table had been set. During the delicious meal, questions and an-swers flew back and forth.

"First I would like to know why you did the Simba Sam act," Freddie asked Bob.

"It all started when I left that package for you at the hotel in Nairobi," Bob replied. "I noticed, after I had given it to the clerk, that

Needles and Soper were spying on me. This meant from then on they would connect you with me. If we had traveled together, it would have been relatively easy for them to follow us. A safari of that size is hard to hide."

"And they would have discovered what you were doing," Bert put in.

"Exactly. In order to throw off the gang, I decided to follow them on my own. Richard knew about it, but we felt the fewer people who were in on the secret, the better."

"You didn't know, either?" Nan asked Jim and Tippy.

"No. But Richard told me not to worry," Jim replied. "I assumed Bob had a secret plan."

"Anyway," Bob continued, "by playing Simba Sam I could let Richard know where the trail had led me. He would then come as my reinforcement with the rest of you, in case I needed it. And, of course, I did!" He smiled and said, "I'm grateful to you children for rescuing me. Without you I'd still be in the hands of the gang!"

Billy looked unhappy. "Dad, why didn't you let me in on it? I worried about Uncle Bob."

Bob Buyanda put his arm around his nephew. "I know, and I'm sorry. But your father and I felt it would be safer if none of you children knew our plans. A couple of times I whistled to get his attention. I wanted to talk to him. That's when you almost found out, Billy."

The boy grinned. "Too bad I didn't catch you."

"I stopped using the signal so you wouldn't," his uncle said.

"It was you playing the pipe in the village, wasn't it?" Nan asked.

"Yes," Bob replied. "I thought you had left already, otherwise I wouldn't have taken the risk."

"And then you spied on Soper during the storm," Flossie went on.

"Right. When I left my father's house that afternoon, I spotted Needles and Soper with their car. It had a flat tire. I listened behind the trees as they talked. When they heard your landrover coming, Soper hid on the floor and Needles hitched a ride with you. Later Soper walked back down into the crater. I followed, but he gave me the slip."

"Did you ever see all the poachers?" Mr. Bobbsey asked.

"Yes, at Amboseli. There are ten including Needles and Soper."

Bert explained his theory about the Hotel Supply Company truck.

"You are probably right," Bob said. "When I was listening to our two friends, I caught the word *van*. Also I heard them mention the *mashua* in the Serengeti. I located it this afternoon. The rest you already know."

Tippy spoke up. "There's one more thing. I overheard the gang talking about their next job. It is to be the biggest one so far."

"When and where is it going to happen?" Bert asked.

"That I don't know. But one man said they would head for the glass house."

"The glass house?" Jim repeated, puzzled.

"I know!" Billy said. "It's probably that big super-modern hotel on the way to Masai Mara Game Reserve. Many of its walls are made of glass."

"That's where we'll go, then," Bob said. "And now," he added, "I think it's time you Bobbseys received the gift that Soper stole from you."

He picked up the package which was on the floor beside Bert, and handed it to Nan.

"But where did you find it?" she asked.

"It was in the *mashua*. Our friends must have dropped it off there."

Nan opened the package. The wrapping had been torn already, because Soper and Needles had looked into it. She pulled out two walkie-talkie sets.

"Oh, they're neat, Bob!" Freddie exclaimed and the others beamed with pleasure.

"I thought my fellow detectives might need these," Bob said. He glanced at his watch.

"We'd better go to bed," he added with a smile. "Tomorrow you must start early for the glass house."

"How about you?" Flossie asked.

"I'll go on ahead in my landrover. But I won't be Simba Sam anymore," Bob said. "Everyone is on to me now."

After the children had thanked the detective for his gift they went to their tents. Bert was about to open the flap when suddenly he stopped and pushed Freddie back.

"Something's in there!"

"Wha-what do you suppose it is?"

"Don't know. It could be some kind of animal."

Now Freddie heard the noise, too. Something was moving around inside their tent!

Freddie was about to turn and run when Bert grasped his arm. "Look!"

A dim light shone through the flap.

"That's no animal," Freddie whispered, trying to be brave. "Somebody's robbing us!"

"I doubt that," Bert said. "We don't have anything that valuable."

"Well, then—" Freddie's voice trailed off, and he flung open the canvas. Loudly, he shouted, *"Stand where you are!"*

A figure was bent over Bert's bed with a flashlight. Danny Rugg! He was plainly frightened by Freddie's command, and the light shook in his hand.

"Ah, well—it's like this—" he stammered.

"He put something in your bed!" Freddie declared, pointing to the disturbed blanket.

Bert yanked back the cover. On the bottom sheet was a clump of long, sharp thorns.

"Out of my way!" Danny cried. He gave Bert a hard push in an effort to leave the tent.

"Oh, no, you don't!" Bert said. He grabbed the other boy, and a wild wrestling match followed.

Danny pushed the palm of his hand into Bert's face, but Bert spun and got a neat headlock on Danny.

"Get him, Bert! Give it to him!" Freddie cried out.

Bert saw a good opportunity. He flipped Danny over his shoulder and the bully landed backside first on the thorny bed.

"Ow!" Danny yelled. He jumped up, pulled out a few thorns and raced out of the tent, right into the arms of Jim.

Jim held the boy tightly, pushed the tent flap aside, and entered. "What's going on here?" he demanded.

"Danny sat on some thorns," Freddie said. "They were in Bert's bed."

Jim plucked more spines from the seat of Danny's pants. "How did they get into Bert's bed?" he asked. "As if I didn't know."

Danny said nothing.

"Are you hurt?" Jim asked him.

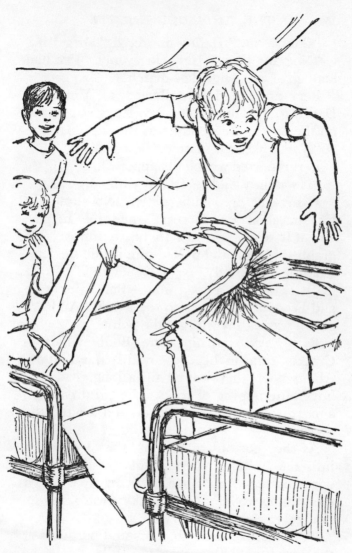

"Ow!" Danny yelled.

"Course not." Danny muttered. "Forget it."

"Not this time," Jim said evenly. "I've had enough of you. Outside—march!"

Bert and Freddie followed as Jim took Danny to the Ruggs' tent. Mr. Rugg was sitting on the porch. He stood up as they approached.

"Now what's the matter?" he asked.

Bert reported what had happened.

"It was only a joke," Danny whined.

His father eyed him coldly. "No allowance for the next four weeks!" he said angrily. "That'll teach you not to be so funny." He grabbed his son and pulled him inside the tent, scolding him loudly.

"It really was a good joke," Bert said, as he and Freddie went back to their tent. "And I'm glad it was Danny who got the point!"

Early next morning the Bobbsey-Barton-Cracker caravan headed toward Masai Mara. About noon they wound up a long road to a huge outcropping of rocks. The children were amazed to see a hotel built on and around the rocks.

As they got out of the car, they looked up into the building through glass-walled corridors. Inside was a tall tree growing up through the dining room and a rocky grotto in the lounge!

"Oh, it's like being indoors and outdoors at the same time!" Flossie said gleefully.

After lunch, Bert looked in the gift shop

for a lion, but none was there. Then he and
Nan took one part of the walkie-talkie set, and
the little twins took the other. Each boy carried the narrow box by a strap over his shoulder. In pairs they went to explore the hotel and
the grounds. On the terrace by the swimming
pool, Flossie stopped in amazement.

"Look! A pink-and-blue lizard!"

Freddie stared, unable to believe his eyes.

"There's another one," cried Flossie, pointing to the rocks beyond. "And another!"

"Bert, Nan, come to the pool!" Freddie said
into the walkie-talkie. "You'll find a surprise!"

"We'll be right there," Bert replied.

Excited, the young twins went on exploring,
meeting Bert and Nan occasionally for an extra
special sight.

Finally, late in the afternoon, they heard
Nan say, "Flossie, Freddie, come down to the
drivers' quarters behind the hotel. Tippy
wants you."

Freddie and Flossie followed directions and
soon arrived in a yard where some men were
working on the motor of a zebra bus. Bert and
Nan stood at the edge of a rocky bluff, petting
the giraffe, while Billy fed her greens. Tippy
was taking their picture.

"Now it's your turn," she said to Freddie
and Flossie. "How would you like to sit on
Crackers' back?"

Flossie giggled. "That'll be fun."

"Okay," Bert said. "Up you go!" He and Nan helped them onto the giraffe's back. Flossie put her arms around her brother's waist.

Just then the bus backfired. The frightened giraffe bolted down the road toward the plain. Flossie and Freddie screamed in fright!

"Stop, Crackers, stop!" Flossie shrieked. But the giraffe only ran faster.

CHAPTER XVII

A FUNNY LIGHTHOUSE

"WHOA, Crackers, whoa!" cried Freddie, and tightened his arms around the giraffe's neck. "Hang on, Flossie!"

The frightened little girl clung to her brother's waist. Her mouth and eyes were clamped shut and only now and then did she blink to see where they were going.

At the bottom of the hill Crackers galloped straight ahead onto the plain. Suddenly, as if out of nowhere, a line of small gazelles came springing across the path of the loping giraffe.

Flossie opened her eyes like saucers. "We're going to hit them!" she screamed. "Crackers, can't you see the gazelles?"

"I wish I knew how to steer a giraffe!" Freddie muttered.

But Crackers knew how to steer herself. She veered and went the opposite way around the hill. On and on she ran with rocking strides. Freddie and Flossie swayed from one side of her slippery back to the other, but managed to hang on.

At last the giraffe slowed to a walk and finally stopped. Flossie gulped and wet her lips. "What a merry-go-round ride!" she said. "Let's get off before Crackers starts running again."

They both jumped to the ground, which seemed a long way down.

"Poor Crackers," said Freddie, petting the trembling animal. "She's scared."

"I am, too," said Flossie. "And Freddie, you know what? I think we're lost."

Holding a hand over her eyes, the little girl gazed out across the vast plain. Herds of animals extended so far away that they seemed like little black dots.

"Don't be silly," Freddie said. "Look behind you. There's the hotel."

But it was far away on the hill. Its glass walls shone like gold in the rays of the setting sun.

"We'll never get back there before dark," Flossie said. "Try the walkie-talkie. If Bert answers, we can tell him where we are."

Freddie tried to work the two-way radio, but he had no luck. "I think it's broken," he said sadly. "We'd better start walking right away."

"But what about Crackers?" Flossie asked, clenching her little fists nervously. "We can't leave her here. A lion might eat her up!"

"I think she'll follow us," Freddie said. "Come on." They headed back the way they had come and, sure enough, the baby giraffe tagged after them as if on an invisible string.

"Crackers is really getting tame," Freddie said. "Soon I'll show her how to do tricks, like standing on her back legs begging for biscuits."

As the three plodded over the dry grass, the huge sun sank lower like a big, glowing ball. No sooner had it disappeared over the horizon, when dusk began to settle over the countryside.

They reached the foot of the hill, but they had still a long way to go. Before them loomed huge broken rocks barring their way.

"We'll never get Crackers over these," said Flossie. "We've got to find the road we came down on."

"But it's way around the other side of the hill," Freddie replied. "Floss, do you have a piece of chewing gum? My mouth is so dry!"

"No. Sorry. And I'm thirsty too," his sister replied.

Suddenly a chill went through Freddie. "Oh oh, what was that noise?"

They listened. The next moment they heard it again. A lion was roaring in the distance!

The twins clung to each other as the roar came again.

"It's getting closer!" Freddie whispered. "We'd better hide."

"But where?" Flossie quavered. She felt her knees knocking together. As they looked anxiously at the hillside, Freddie spotted a narrow crevice between two great blocks of rock.

"In there!" he commanded. "Come on, Crackers!"

The giraffe's red Christmas bow had slipped down and hung bedraggled around the base of her neck. Grabbing it, Freddie led Crackers into the crevice, with Flossie following.

"It's going to be a tight squeeze," the girl whispered. The lion roared again, even closer.

"We've got to get her in!" Freddie said. He slipped sidewise into the crack, pulling the giraffe with all his might.

Flossie pushed from the back. For a moment, Crackers was stuck.

"Harder! Push harder!" Freddie cried.

"I can't!" Flossie said.

"Then give her a slap!"

Flossie's hand was not very large, nor could she hit very hard. But the sudden slap on Crackers' hind leg startled the animal. She jerked forward and freed herself.

A few feet ahead, the crevice widened into a small chamber with a narrow opening in the roof.

"We made it!" Freddie sighed with relief.

"Yes, but look!" his sister said, pointing upward. "Crackers' head sticks out over the top!"

"Get down!" Freddie said. He tugged at the ribbon. Crackers, however, gazed calmly out over the rocks, as if nothing in the world could harm her.

Flossie's hand went to her pocket. Good! There were two crackers left. She held them up.

"Here's a treat for you," she said to the giraffe. Crackers liked the idea. She bent her neck and while she ate the cracker, Freddie fastened the ribbon firmly under her head again. He held onto it, trying to keep her out of sight. But Crackers strained and strained to lift her head.

"Don't you understand?" Flossie said, stamping her foot. "If the lion sees you here, he'll come and eat you—and us, too!"

"Do you really think the lion could make it in here?" Freddie whispered.

Flossie tried to be brave. She had heard her mother talk about positive thinking. "I don't think so," she said. "The entrance is kind of narrow."

"Well, *we* got in!"

Again the roar sounded. This time it came from somewhere above them. The trembling children held tightly to the giraffe's neck. Now, sensing real danger, Crackers began to struggle.

"Stop, please stop!" Flossie cried out. "If you run away now, you'll get eaten!"

"Oh, if only somebody would find us," Freddie said. He glanced up and uttered a sharp cry. Looking down into the crevice was a large lion. He snarled and swiped at them with an outstretched paw. Terrified, Flossie started screaming.

"Get down," Freddie cried. Holding tight to the giraffe's ribbon, he dropped to the rocky floor and pulled his sister with him. "Go away!" he yelled at the lion.

Meanwhile, Bert, Nan, and Billy were on the roof of the hotel. They took turns looking through binoculars that the hotel manager had lent them. Back and forth they scanned the plains, trying to pick out a small giraffe and two children. But they had no luck at all.

"What are those three black dots way out there?" Billy asked as Bert peered through the binoculars.

"They're buffalo," Bert replied gloomily. "I can see something else," he added. "Take a look."

The African's eyes swept over the desolate scene. "Oh, yes. That's my father and Jim and Tippy in the landrover. And hey, one, two, three, four, five, six ranger cars are out there searching for Freddie and Flossie. They'll be sure to find them."

"They'd better do it soon," said Nan in a

"Go away!" Freddie yelled at the lion.

worried voice. "It's getting dark. Try the walkie-talkie again, Bert."

"Okay. But I couldn't get an answer before. Maybe the set fell off Freddie when Crackers was running away."

Bert adjusted the dial. "Freddie, do you read me? Freddie, do you read me?"

The radio squawked and whistled, and suddenly there was Freddie's voice. "I read you, Bert. Help!"

Flossie took the set. "A lion almost got us, but he's gone now."

"Where are you? Out on the plain?"

"No. We were on the way home when we got blocked by all these big rocks. It's impossible to get Crackers over them."

"Here, let me talk," Billy said. "Flossie, tell me exactly where you are."

She did.

"I know where those rocks are," Billy said. "I used to camp there with my dad. Hang on now and don't be scared. We'll get you!"

"All right," Flossie quavered. "But hurry. It's getting cold."

Bert took the radio from Billy and turned it off. "No wonder no one's found them. They're all searching on the plain."

"What's the quickest way to reach the crevice?" Nan asked.

"We'll climb down the hill below the swimming pool," Billy said. "Here, take a look

through the binoculars. See those black boulders? That's where they are."

The twins gazed through the instrument.

"Come on," Billy urged. "Let's go."

"First we must get word to the searchers,"
Nan said.

"Right. The hotel manager can flash the location over the radio," Billy declared.

"If there's a landrover available, maybe
someone can drive us," Bert suggested.

The three went to the manager's desk, but
he was not there.

"Oh dear," said Nan, "I wonder where he
is." They ran along the corridors looking for
him. Bert finally spotted him, and when the
boy had blurted out his story, the manager
hastened back to his desk. "Sorry, I don't have
any cars available," he said. "They're all out
searching. But I'll send a message to the rangers."

"Okay. We'll go on ahead," Billy said.

Bert and Nan followed the African boy over
the edge of the hill. They all carried flashlights,
and Bert had his rope. Billy moved swiftly
from one large rock to another. Twenty minutes later the trio paused on a ledge and peered
down on the slope below.

"There they are!" Nan said suddenly. "I see
Crackers!"

She pointed to the giraffe's head sticking
out from the jumble of rocks.

It did not take the nimble rescuers very long to reach the crevice. One by one, they squeezed into it. Nan hugged her brother and sister.

"Oh, Nan, we were so scared!" Flossie cried.

Excitedly the young twins told about their adventure with the lion.

"Flossie screamed," Freddie said, "and I threw stones. Then the lion ran away."

"And afterwards," Flossie added, "poor Crackers was so restless that we had to let her stick her head up for a while."

"What happened to your walkie-talkie?" Bert asked. "We tried to raise you for a long time, but couldn't."

Freddie explained that the antenna had come loose. "At first I didn't realize it and thought the set was broken, but finally I saw it and fixed it. All I had to do was to screw it in tighter."

Bert looked about the hiding place. "We'd better block the entrance to the plain," he said. He spied a large boulder on one side. He and Nan and Billy pushed it in front of the crack.

"And we must keep a pile of stones handy, too," Nan said, "in case we have any more visitors up above."

"I don't think a lion could get down here," Bert said. "The opening is too small."

"But a cheetah could," Billy said quietly.

"Anyhow, once word is flashed to the rang-

ers, they'll be here soon, you can bet on that,"
Nan stated.

It was decided that some sort of signal was
needed to help the searchers locate them.

"We could put a light up on the edge of the
crevice," Nan suggested.

"It wouldn't do much good," Bert said.
"There are other rocks blocking the view
from the plain."

"I have an idea," Freddie said. "Let Crackers put her head up and hold the light. We can
tie it under her chin with the ribbon."

"That's neat," said Nan.

"But what about the lion?" Bert worried.

Billy had a solution for that. "Let's gather
stones, then throw them out in all directions.
If there's a lion anywhere near us, he'll run!"

Bert pulled down the giraffe's neck, and
Billy tied a flashlight around it. Then he gave
her a pat. "Now stand up straight!"

Bert released the animal and Crackers lifted
her head high out of the crevice.

"She's our lighthouse," Freddie said.

"Whoever heard of a yellow lighthouse with
black spots, wearing a red ribbon?" Flossie
giggled.

The youngsters were so excited by their im-
pending rescue that time moved by quickly.
Finally Billy glanced at his watch. "We've
been here twenty minutes already," he said.
"They should have reached us by now."

Just then the roar of a motor drifted over the plain.

"Here they come!" Nan cried out.

The sound ceased outside the cleft. The older children rolled the boulder aside as fast as they could.

"We're in here!" Freddie cried out, flashing his light at the entrance. The next moment a man appeared. The light shone directly into his face.

It was Mr. Needles!

CHAPTER XVIII

THE HIPPO POOL

NEEDLES pushed into the cleft with a sneer on his face. He was followed by a blond man with a scraggly beard and several others.

"But—but we were supposed to be rescued," Flossie said.

"Oh, yes. We know that," Needles said. "However, Mr. Soper neatly foiled your plan."

"How?" Bert asked.

"He overheard you at the hotel telling the manager to give the rangers the location of this hideout. Soper bopped him on the head before he could broadcast anything, then he called us on our special wavelength and told us where you were!"

"Now that we've caught the snoopers," said

the blond-bearded man, "what'll we do with them?"

"I know a certain cave," Needles replied. "We'll put them in there until we're finished. We've got one big job left, and I don't want them to interfere with this one!"

"I'd rather let them go. It's too risky to fool with them."

"You're an idiot, Jones," retorted Needles. "If these five are missing, everyone will be busy looking for them. They won't have time to think about poachers. We'll get the hippos tomorrow night in perfect safety."

"Well, you're the boss," Jones said, shaking his head.

The Bobbseys were stunned. Was Needles the head of the gang?

"So you are the mastermind, Mr. Needles!" Bert exclaimed.

"Of course. Didn't you know that? Soper and I, we run the Leopard Gang. We travel around the world getting contracts, have the animals captured, and deliver them."

"We'd better get out of here before someone sees the flashlight on the giraffe," Jones put in.

"Everyone in the truck!" Needles commanded.

Just then came the sound of cars approaching.

"The rangers!" Needles cried. "Forget the kids and get out of here!"

The poachers dashed to their truck. With lights out, it sped into the plain. Seconds later, three landrovers screeched to a halt in front of the crevice.

The children came out and saw Tippy jump out first.

"Are you all right?" she called as Jim and Richard followed.

"Yes!" Billy replied. "But there go the poachers!"

Richard acted instantly. He motioned to the other two landrovers to follow the speeding truck, which was now out of sight in the darkness.

"Bob is in one of those cars," he said, "and several rangers in the other. Maybe they can catch the crooks yet. Did anybody get hurt?"

"No," Bert said. "But it's a good thing you came in time. They were going to stick us in a cave!"

Richard nodded. "Get into the car," he said. "It's not safe here."

"What about Crackers?" Flossie spoke up.

"We'll take her, too. She can put her head out. We'll raise the roof. It'll be crowded, but we'll manage."

Everyone piled in, and Richard drove off. An explosion boomed out over the silent plain before they were halfway to The Lodge. It was followed by three more blasts.

"What was that?" Nan exclaimed.

"Maybe the rangers are shooting the poachers," Freddie said.

"No. That was no rifle shot," Jim said. "It sounded more like a bomb to me!" His voice was tense.

When they arrived at the hotel, Billy took Crackers to her pen, while the others hurried to the manager's office. He wore a bandage on his head where Soper had hit him. As he told his story, Bob Buyanda arrived.

"Any luck?" Jim asked.

Bob shook his head. "Those poachers had a real arsenal with them. Tossed delayed action bombs out of their car. One of our landrovers was disabled and one man slightly hurt, so we had to quit."

"We're not making a great record for ourselves as poacher catchers," Richard muttered.

"Oh, but we'll get them!" Flossie chirped.

The ranger smiled. "You never give up, do you?"

"Nope," Freddie said. "Besides, Mr. Needles said he wants to pull off another job tomorrow night."

"Where?" Bob asked.

Freddie shrugged. "He didn't say. But he mentioned hippos."

"I know!" Tippy cried out. "When I was in

the *mashua,* I heard them say something about the hippo pool!"

"But where is it?" Bert asked.

"There are several. But one is not far from here," Bob Buyanda said. "It's a wide part in the river. A great place for a poacher raid!"

"We must set a trap for the gang!" Richard declared. "I'll get in touch with the patrol."

"We want to help, too!" Bert said eagerly.

"You may be the lookouts," Richard said. "The roundup itself is a job for the rangers. These are real rough people."

"The hippo pool is closest to the Masai Mara Lodge," Bob said. "I'll meet you there tomorrow."

"Wait a minute," Jim said. "Maybe we shouldn't go there. Suppose the crooks see us. Then they'll know we're on their trail."

Bob was thoughtful for a moment. Then he said, "Setting up camp is too dangerous with the children. I wouldn't want to risk it. Besides, since the poachers have it all planned, I doubt that they will go to the lodge."

After their exciting adventure, all the children slept well. In the morning they climbed eagerly into the landrover with Crackers trailing behind. Shortly before noon they reached a stone gatehouse and drove into a circular driveway to a handsome lodge with a high-peaked roof. Nearby on a wide green lawn was a long row of guest houses.

As soon as the party was settled in two of them, Bob Buyanda arrived and everyone got together for lunch. Afterwards they retreated into one guest house to make plans. Bob and Richard outlined what they would do and Billy said, "I'll teach you the signal we'll use."

Puckering his lips, he gave a loud, double whistle. "That's the call of the freckled nightjar."

"A freckled nightie?" asked Flossie and everyone laughed.

"No. A freckled nightjar," the African boy explained, "is one of our local birds here."

The twins and Tippy practiced until they could imitate the unusual sound perfectly. When dusk settled over the great quiet stretch of Africa, the Bobbseys and their friends drove to the hippo pool.

They stopped on a bluff overlooking the wide part of the river. Down below, at least a dozen of the big creatures lay on a sandbar. In the water were several tiny black backs. Now and then a large, pinkish snout appeared on the surface.

"Lots of other animals come here at night to drink," Billy said. "The poachers'll be after all of them."

Richard got out of the landrover and said, "Bob and six rangers are already hiding. Take your positions now."

As planned, he and Jim started down a path

to the riverbank. Tippy, Freddie, and Flossie stayed in the landrover, which was well shielded by bushes and trees. Bert, Nan, and Billy, meanwhile, crept into the thickets near the top of the trail. Hidden there already was a large searchlight.

Then came the long, tedious time of waiting. The moon was rising when they finally heard three clear double whistles from the road. It set their hearts to pounding.

"The poachers are coming," Bert whispered. Dark figures appeared at the top of the path. As each man went down, Nan gave the nightjar call—ten times. In a minute, Bob returned the signal.

Bert flicked the switch of the giant searchlight, and the riverbank was flooded with light. The poachers were caught in the brilliant glare. Bob, Jim, Richard, and six rangers stepped out of the brush.

"You're covered with rifles!" Bob Buyanda snapped. "Put down your weapons!"

The men dropped their guns.

"We've been tricked!" Needles cried hoarsely. "Those Bobbsey Twins, I'll bet!" Soper just stared, speechless.

The surprised criminals were swiftly handcuffed before the older children reached the bank. Several minutes later Freddie, Flossie, and Tippy appeared.

Jones shook his head and grumbled, "I told

"The poachers are coming!" Bert whispered.

you we shouldn't have done this! They were too hot on our trail!"

Now the rangers began to question their prisoners. Bob Buyanda searched the leaders and pulled a small black book from Needles' jacket.

He glanced at it and smiled. "A list of all your spies at the various hotels! That'll help us round up all your henchmen in the morning, Needles."

Now the jigsaw puzzle of the events of the last week fell into place. Needles admitted that it was he who had pushed Jim down the cliff at Manyara. Soper had tied Nan into the blanket.

"Didn't you know Billy and I were there, too?" Bert asked.

"No," Needles grumbled. "Or else we wouldn't have signaled that night!"

It was those two men Flossie had later overheard in the hallway. "You must have been planning that trick with the walking bush," Flossie said.

"We wanted to scare you enough so you'd stay indoors at night," Soper admitted. "I held the bush and meowed."

"One thing I don't understand," Billy spoke up, "is why didn't you strike that night the Italians came? Everything was all set, wasn't it?"

But with the busload of Romans had come more unexpected reinforcements for the patrol. Needles had found out about it and had not given the signal.

"How did you work your signals, anyway?" Tippy asked.

"Morse code," Needles muttered. "That's how I told them when and where to strike."

"And the lion carvings in the hotel gift shops told the day and the area where the strike should take place?" Nan asked.

Needles nodded glumly.

"Did you tell your men to fool the guards at Amboseli Game Reserve?" Richard asked.

Needles shook his head. "That was Jones's idea. I didn't expect the patrol to be in that spot."

"Every place was swarming with rangers lately," Jones added. "Even when we got the signal to strike we had to be careful."

"Why did you steal the zebra bus?" Nan asked. "You had two trucks already."

"One of them had broken down," Soper admitted.

Tippy had been scrutinizing the men and now spoke up. "This is the fake ranger who came to the hotel and kidnapped me!" she said, pointing to a medium-sized man with close-cropped hair.

"Well, that just about wraps up our inquiry," Bob Buyanda said. "I will personally take these men to Nairobi, and I thank you all for helping to solve the case!"

He shook hands with the Americans while the rangers herded the poachers into their two trucks and locked them in the back. Then Bob slid behind the wheel of one truck. Another ranger offered to drive the second vehicle, while the rest went along to guard the prisoners.

The children and their friends drove back to the Masai Mara Lodge. On the way, Jim said, "This is the end of our safari. Tomorrow your parents will come here and we'll all go back. But there's one more thing we have to do."

"What's that?" Nan asked.

"Take Crackers back to her birthplace," Billy told her.

Next morning they set out on their last mission. A mile from the lodge, Flossie cried out, "Look at all the giraffes!"

Richard stopped the car. "Here's where we say good-by to Crackers."

Everyone got out and walked around to the trailer. Jim opened it, and the girls coaxed their pet out with a salty cracker.

Billy led the baby close to the big giraffes, who stared curiously at the newcomer.

Quietly the children climbed back into the landrover.

"*Kwaheri,* Crackers," Freddie said sadly.

As they slowly drove off, the little giraffe

started to tag along after them. But a large giraffe nudged Crackers firmly toward a tree. She took a mouthful of leaves, then another, and another. The twins watched until they could not see her any more.

"Oh," said Flossie with a sigh. "We'll miss Crackers. I wish she could have been at our farewell party tonight."

"Cheer up," said Nan. "She's at a welcome-home party right now!"

"Yes," said Bert, grinning. "She's enjoying real giraffe food!"

"And that's very *zuri* for her!" Freddie added.